New York Times & *USA Today* Bestselling Author
KENDALL RYAN

Dear Jane

Content Editing by
Elaine York

Copy Editing by
Pam Berehulke

Cover Design and Formating by
Uplifting Designs

About the Book

I broke her heart ten years ago and left town.

She hates me, and rightly so. It doesn't matter that the rest of the country loves me, that I'm a starting quarterback with a multimillion-dollar contract. Because when I look in the mirror, all I see is a failure who was too young—and too afraid—to fight for what I wanted.

But I'm not that guy anymore, and all I need is one shot to convince her.

• • •

He has no idea what happened after he left. And now I'm supposed to work alongside him like we don't have this huge, messy history?

But I'm older now, wiser, and I won't let anything stand in my way of doing a good job for this league. Not even one overpaid, arrogant player who thinks we're going to kiss and make up.

News flash, buddy: I am over you.

CHAPTER One

Jane

Nine times out of ten, when I tell people I work for a professional football team, they try to call my bluff. Usually, they make me repeat myself—"Come again?"—like they misheard me and I'm actually a manicurist or a dog sitter or something. Sometimes, they'll quiz me on players' jersey numbers or specific game plays, all of which I can answer without batting an eye.

I guess I can't blame people when they don't expect a pint-sized girl who loves heels and lipstick to be working in an industry of huge, muscular men pummeling each other into the turf for entertainment, but this world is all I know.

I was raised in a home where it was practically

law that I was on the couch to watch the Hawks game every Sunday afternoon, and my love affair with the sport hasn't stopped since. The fact that I get to work for the team I've been cheering for since I was in diapers seems almost too good to be true. Not to mention the fact that I have the most foolproof pickup line in any sports bar ever. Between traveling the country with the team and brushing shoulders with sports legends, football is my religion.

And then there are days like today. With all the paperwork falling off of my desk, you'd think a tornado hit the Chicago area and touched down only in my office. The season is starting in just over a week, and my to-do list is longer than the whole length of the field.

It doesn't help that Mr. Flores, the general manager of the Hawks, is offsite all day at a meeting, so as his assistant manager, I'll be picking up his slack. As if that weren't enough, there's a huge press conference tomorrow to get ready for. This day is going to require a refill on my coffee and a whole lot of gangster rap.

I slip in my earbuds and put on my best game face, envisioning the frozen margarita I'm going to order later as a reward. And then, just as I'm getting into the zone, there's a knock on my office door and in walks the head coach. Or as I like to call him, Dad.

"Hey, sweetheart, is it okay if I bother you for a second?"

Despite what a lot of people think, my dad didn't get me this job. He probably could have if I'd let him, but I've never wanted to use Dad's position to my advantage. I'm perfectly capable of paving my own way without being given a leg up. So I served my time selling tickets before I eventually worked my way up to having my own office.

"Sure, if it's important," I say, glancing at my watch. It feels rude not to make a little time for my own father, even if I am totally swamped today.

Dad shuts the door behind him and plops down in the faux leather armchair across from my desk. "I'd say it's pretty important," he says, dodging direct eye contact with me. "But you're not going to like it."

I survey my mountain of paperwork and give Dad my best *bring it on* smile. With everything on my plate today, I came in to work ready for battle. It would take something pretty catastrophic to throw me off my game.

"We're bringing on a new player."

My eyebrows perk up in interest. It's pretty unheard of to make changes to the roster this close to the start of the season. Plus, if the Hawks have been eyeing a potential new player, I should have been one of the first people to know.

"Really? Who?" I prop my chin in my hands, leaning in like a high school girl ready for the hot gossip.

Dad lets out a long breath, his lips tensing as he nervously adjusts his Hawks cap. "It's, uh . . . it's Weston Chase."

My stomach bottoms out. I must have misheard him. There's no way my dad just told me that Weston Chase—my first and only long-term boyfriend, the star of our school's football team who shattered my heart and touchdown-danced all over the pieces—is joining the Hawks.

"Excuse me?" I'll give him a chance to repeat himself and prove that I must be losing my hearing at an alarmingly young age. Please, *please* say another name. Any other name.

"Weston Chase. You remember him, right?"

"Are . . . are you k-kidding me?" I manage to

sputter as my whole body locks up. My heart literally stutters in my chest like it's threatening to stop.

This has to be a joke, some kind of preseason prank the guys on the team put him up to. Weston Chase is a thing of the past, a heartbreak nightmare I have left way, way behind me. What sort of terrible karma would bring him to the Hawks?

"I know it's not great," Dad says in what feels like the biggest understatement in history.

Rainy days aren't great. Fast food tacos aren't great. My ex-boyfriend stomping back into my life and turning my dream job into a nightmare? That's a fricking disaster.

Dad has no idea what really happened with Wes and me all those years ago. Almost no one knows. About the baby, about my heartbreak . . .

"I wanted to keep it under wraps in case it didn't end up happening," Dad explains, fiddling with the fraying edge of his hat. "I didn't want you getting all worked up for nothing. But Weston is meeting with the general manager today, so it looks like things are pretty set in stone. We're going to announce him as our new quarterback at tomorrow's press conference."

Tomorrow? So I have less than twenty-four

hours to prepare to face the douchebag who shattered my heart into a million tiny pieces?

Just two minutes ago, I was ready for the day to fly by, eyeing my frozen margarita on the other side, and now I wish everything would just freeze for a second so I can stop my head from spinning. It's not like I didn't know Wes was a professional football player, no matter how hard I tried to block out any and all news about him since he was first drafted.

"Are you going to be all right, sweetie?" Dad asks.

I realize I haven't said anything as I stare into space. I've got to get a hold of myself.

"I don't really have a choice, do I?" I grumble through clenched teeth, rubbing my temples to ward off an impending stress headache.

"I'm sorry, sweetheart. I just figured it was best you heard it from me. I didn't want you bumping into the guy for the first time in almost ten years without a little fair warning."

Holy shit, almost ten years? Has it really been that long? Nearly a whole decade since I've seen Weston Chase.

It feels like just last week we were sneaking a bottle of wine out of his mom's pantry and making toasts to his football scholarship in his backyard. That was the night before he left for college. We caught our first buzz off that wine, kissing and promising we'd talk on the phone every single day until he came home for Thanksgiving.

It seemed so perfect at the time. Now it just feels like a load of bullshit.

"Why the Hawks?" I ask, waving off that memory like the sour smell of a used jockstrap. "Can't he go play for literally any other team?"

"He *was* playing for another team. We're getting him from Philadelphia."

"And he couldn't have stayed there?" I snap, my sassy tone biting.

"Jane, let me get through the whole story, would you?"

I let my gaze fall apologetically to my desk, like a puppy who just got scolded. I shouldn't be taking out my frustration on Dad. The truth is, I'm glad he thought to come to me about this.

He's quiet for a second, drumming his fingers on the arm of his chair, probably trying to figure out the best way to go about it. When he speaks again, his tone is soft and careful, like he's treading through a minefield, worried I may explode at any second.

And I just might.

"You know our starting quarterback is out for the season with that ACL injury. Yeah, we have our backup, but you and I both know he's not good enough to carry us to the playoffs. And things weren't going great for Wes in Philadelphia. His fiancée cheated on him with their star linebacker. It was a real messy situation, Jane. He needed out of there, stat."

Is it bad that hearing that Wes got cheated on makes the corner of my mouth threaten a smile? I try to keep my best poker face, act like I'm not secretly pleased that Weston Chase got what was coming to him, but Dad notices the snicker I'm holding back.

"Look, I don't know exactly what went down between you two," Dad confesses, putting his hands out in front of him in surrender, "and I don't want to know. Some things a father just doesn't need to know about. But I know you walked away with a pretty bruised-up heart."

More like limped away, or maybe crawled. Dad is making it sound like Wes and I ended on polite terms, like I made a full recovery after a few pints of brownie ice cream and a good cry or two. I wish it were that simple.

"It was . . . complicated," I admit, my throat going tight. I squeeze my eyes shut, pulling myself together the best I can. One way or another, I'm going to have to get through this. After a deep breath, I add, "But it was a long time ago."

He considers this for a moment, studying me closely. "You want me to bench him?"

I smile at Dad and shake my head. You don't bench players like Wes. Not in a million years. There are football players and then there are quarterbacks, and among the country's most elite quarterbacks, Weston Chase is firmly at the top. It would be crime against football to bench him. Dad knows that as well as I do, but it's still sweet of him to offer.

Dad gives me his signature half smile that I know means he's proud of me. "You've got this, kiddo. And besides, this really is the best place for Wes. Back close to home, close to his mom and all. Plus, our backup kicker, Colin, is an old college buddy of his. He's the one who gave us the lead on recruiting Wes to the Hawks. I guess they used to live together, and he—"

I hold up a hand in protest, cutting Dad off from sharing any more details of Wes's life. If I'm going to be professional with him, I've got to stay far, far away from any of the personal stuff. "Need-to-know basis, Dad."

He gives me one firm nod. "Understood." He drums his fingers one last time on the chair and I glance at my watch again, silently ushering him out the door and ending this father-daughter moment.

"Well, I guess I'll leave you to scale your mountain of paperwork," he teases, gesturing to the chaos that is my desk.

I mentally thank my busy schedule for providing me with a good distraction from this Wes stuff.

"Thanks, Dad. Love you," I say, wiggling one hand in a wave as the other reaches for my to-do list.

Just as Dad twists the doorknob, he pivots and adds one final thought. "This might turn out to be a good thing, sweetheart. You never know."

I fake an enthusiastic smile, then grab a pen and scrawl one final item onto my to-do list.

Stay far, far away from Weston Chase.

• • •

One of the best things about being the Hawks' assistant manager is that the spotlight is never on me. I have no interest in being the center of attention, so I'm happy to slip out of the shot when the cameras flash on Mr. Flores. And with the announcement of our last-minute roster addition, every reporter, blogger, and talk-show host in the country is clamoring to get a quote from him. Probably for the best that no one cares to hear my opinion on the matter, because I'd have a few choice words on our new player if any news outlet gave me the mic. And I don't particularly feel like getting fired today.

After our usual pre-press-conference routine of running a few practice questions in his office, Mr. Flores pulls two ties out of his lower desk drawer, holding each one up to his chest so I can get the full image.

"I know I'm being ridiculous," he admits. "But you know the room is going to be packed with reporters from every major news outlet."

Glad I'm not the only one dressing to impress today, I smirk, pointing to the navy tie in Flores's right hand. "Team colors."

I've got on my personal brand of battle gear—high-rise black skinny jeans with an army-green blazer, dark red lipstick, and the sexiest underwear I own. Not that anyone is going to see this little lacy black number, but just knowing I have it on is a major confidence boost.

And this press conference is going to take every ounce of confidence I can dredge up. I have half a mind to throw on a football helmet too, so maybe I can get through this press conference without Wes noticing or recognizing me, but I know I can't hide from him forever. If I don't face him now, I'll just have to do it tomorrow or the next day. No use putting it off.

And the last thing I want him thinking is that I'm cowering in the corner, fearful of him.

Mr. Flores gets one last look at himself in the reflection of his window, smoothing out his suit jacket and giving himself a nod of approval. "Ready?" he asks, tightening the knot of his tie.

"As I'll ever be."

I follow Mr. Flores down the hall to the elevator, which takes us straight to the media room. As soon as the elevator doors slide open, the familiar flash of cameras greets us. I recognize all the usual photographers but see at least a dozen unfamiliar faces. I guess bringing on Wes really is a big deal. A $50 million big deal, if the rumors are true.

As Mr. Flores heads to the table to take his seat next to my dad, I slip to the back of the room. There's one empty chair onstage, but I know it won't stay empty for long. As if on cue, the locker-room door swings open, and in walks my own personal blast from the past.

It pains me to say it, but Weston Chase looks damn good. Tall. Insanely fit. Cocky swagger.

But this isn't the high school heartthrob I fell for anymore. Ten years of weightlifting and endurance training have done him quite a few favors. He still has the same short brown hair, which is styled with gel, and his tight smile is as familiar as ever. All the things I loved about him haven't changed, and I'm sure that means all the things I've hated are the same too.

I inhale sharply and watch as he stalks toward his spot between my father and Mr. Flores. He holds up one hand to greet the crowd before taking his seat. Dad gives him a friendly slap on one broad, sculpted shoulder, which makes me twitch a little. It feels like a high school football game all over again with Wes in his jersey and me in the crowd.

And then it happens. He sees me. I should have blended in with the reporters, or at least kept from staring at him for so long, but it's too late. He spotted me, and he's not looking away.

Shit. Fixing my focus on Dad, I force myself to do my best impression of someone who gives zero fucks about Wes's presence in this room, nodding along with my dad's answers as if I'm catching more than every third word. I sure as hell can't focus with Weston Chase's stare burning a hole in my cheek.

Even as the reporters turn their attention to Wes, I never once feel his eyes drift away from me. He answers in that same low, maple-syrup voice that I used to love. That same deep voice that used to whisper against my neck how beautiful I was, how good I felt. It makes every hair on my body stand at attention.

Don't. You. Dare. Look. At. Him.

I force another breath into my oxygen-deprived lungs and try not to act like my whole world wasn't just shaken.

What I'm sure is a twenty-minute press conference feels like a century, but things finally come to a close. As the room clears out, Wes disappears into the locker room in the blink of an eye. Finally.

I take a much-needed pull of oxygen. I did it. I survived.

"Jane! Over here!"

I scan the room for the source of the request—it's Mr. Flores. He waves me over as he chats one-on-one with a perky blond reporter.

"Jane, can you do me a favor? This woman from the *Times* wants to chat with Colin Crosley, number forty-one. He was Weston's roommate in college, and she's looking for a quote. Could you pull him out of the locker room for me?"

I gulp down the enormous lump in my throat. The locker room? You mean the place Wes *just* walked into?

I rack my brain for any excuse not to go in there, but I've got nothing that Flores would buy. He sends me in there to give messages to the players at least once a week. As the coach's daughter, I'm practically a sister to those guys, and half of them have underwear sponsorships anyway, so all of America has seen them almost naked. It's never been a big deal.

Until now.

Now it feels like a very, very big deal.

"I've got it," I manage to say through a forced smile.

I square my shoulders, preparing myself for whatever I'm about to walk into. Just get in there, be professional, and get out. Nothing you can't handle. Maybe you won't even run into "he who shall not be named."

I push open the heavy steel door and wander through the short hallway to the locker-room door. The double doors mean that no one can accidentally steal a peek of a player indisposed, but they also mean you can't see who's coming around the corner.

I must have pushed a little too hard on the door because it swings all the way open, thwacking a nearby player. "Oops, sorry!"

And by a nearby player, I mean Weston Chase. And by Weston Chase, I mean Weston Chase wearing nothing but a pair of athletic shorts slung low on his trim hips. Just my luck.

I can't stop my mouth from falling open a little. I thought he looked good up there in his jersey, but that was nothing compared to the Greek god standing in front of me.

My gaze wanders from his broad shoulders to his smooth, defined pecs and perfectly carved abs. It's like all the air's been sucked from the room, and I can't even speak. Definitely can't raise my head and look into his eyes. I don't want to know what I'd find there. Amusement maybe? Curiosity about me, about the woman I've grown into? Or worse, indifference?

I swivel on the heels of my leather pumps, desperately looking for someone else, anyone else, I can talk to.

"What's up, Jane?" It's Alex, our best linebacker, one of my closest friends on the team.

Thank God.

"Hi, Alex." I sigh, every molecule in my body dripping with relief. "Could you send Colin out? The press wants a quote from him about . . ." I swallow the rest of the sentence, clenching my hands into fists to keep them from shaking.

Alex looks around the locker room, scratching at the scruff on his cheek. "Wes, have you seen Colin?"

Really, Alex? Really? Give me a fricking break. I don't dare stick around to catch Wes's response. I've got to get out of here.

"Just find him and send him out ASAP," I rattle off in my sternest assistant-manager voice.

Alex shoots me a concerned look, his eyebrows knitting together. "You okay, Jane?"

I don't bother answering, too worried that I might tell the truth. Instead, I push on the locker-room door and strut out with whatever pride I have remaining.

One press conference down, an entire season to go.

CHAPTER *Two*

Weston

Holy hell, the years have been good to her.

That's the first thought that flits through my brain.

The second is *little Janie Royce isn't so little anymore*. She's all woman now, even more stunning than the knockout girl I first fell for so long ago. Her clothes hug every generous curve of her petite frame. Her honey-colored hair looks as temptingly silky as I remember. I used to run my fingers through it every time I kissed her, and the sight makes me itch to feel it again.

She carries herself with a confidence that makes her five feet three inches seem much taller. She's totally in her element here, not at all intimidated by the pack of huge, musclebound men that crowd the locker room. They clearly know she's just as much their boss as her dad is. It's obvious that she's earned their respect, and something inside me is pleased by that knowledge.

I'm so busy gawking I can barely hear what she's saying to Alex Ivan, the team's linebacker. I busy myself collecting my shower stuff so she won't notice me standing there staring at her like a moron, but I still can't stop myself from sneaking glances.

She's dressed in black skinny jeans that hug her ass in the most distracting and mouthwatering way, and her hands move as she talks. Smirking, I remember how animated she used to get when she was passionate about something, and wonder what it is that's got her so riled up. It's obviously not me. She all but shoved past me with barely a second glance—like I didn't matter at all, like she wasn't in love with me all those years ago. Her dismissal stung more than I expected it to.

All too soon, she finishes and marches out of the locker room. My gaze stays glued to the sway of her round hips until the door swings shut behind her.

Just like in high school . . . whenever she's near, all I can see is her. But she clearly doesn't feel the same way about me anymore. Other than quick glances at the press conference and when she crashed into me just now, she's barely looked at me, let alone talked to me. She's acting like I don't exist. It's the polar opposite of the fawning adoration most women usually offer me, even when they don't know I'm a starting quarterback.

No, Jane is all business, wearing her job title like a mask. It's almost enough to make me wonder if she's forgotten who I am . . . what we used to be. But her eyes could have frozen a volcano solid. She remembers me, all right, and not fondly.

I'm not an idiot—I knew it might be a little awkward joining a team where the assistant manager is my high school sweetheart. We were each other's first loves, first everything. We gave each other our virginity, and after that, she gave me her whole heart. I gladly took it, and our breakup wasn't easy.

At nineteen, freshly recruited to a top state school on a football scholarship, I was way too dumb and immature to juggle a long-distance relationship along with the pressures of competing at a college level and not flunking my classes. The teenage romance we'd believed would last forever ended up falling apart.

But after ten frigging years, I didn't expect such naked hostility. I didn't think our history would still be sitting right there on the surface, raw and ugly . . . especially since Jane was the one who dumped me.

So, why is she still so pissed off? And what the hell should I do about it?

Even after I've showered, toweled off, and dressed, I'm no closer to an answer. It doesn't help that her beauty is still spinning in my mind, or the thought that I'll have to work closely with her for the foreseeable future.

"You almost ready to head home?" Colin asks.

"Huh?" I look up to find him standing next to me; I didn't notice him walk up. "Oh, yeah. Just gotta put on my shoes. You're already done with the reporter?"

"I've been done for twenty minutes, dude. Hurry up so we can get some dinner before my stomach eats itself."

On our way through the exit hall, I spot Jane talking to an old man in a gray custodian uniform. Her professionalism has softened. She's smiling, her blue eyes sparkling, just chatting away, and I feel a stab of jealousy that she pays more attention to the damn janitor than me.

Oh, come on, Wes, you're being stupid.

She's the assistant manager—maybe she's discussing a work issue with him. Hell, even if she isn't, she's a grown-ass woman who can talk or *not talk* to anyone she wants. But it still stings, and suddenly I need to know just how far she's going to take this cold-shoulder routine.

As Colin and I walk past, I offer a friendly, but not too friendly, "Good night."

She blinks at me, her smile vanishing into a carefully neutral expression. She lifts her chin. "Weston," she replies, her voice clipped and formal, before striding away.

My full name. When she's always called me Wes.

Fuck . . . I don't like this at all.

• • •

Colin drives us to his house. I sold my car in Philly and haven't gotten a chance to buy a new one yet; guess I need to rent one. All I brought to Illinois was a couple of duffel bags of clothes.

I take advantage of riding shotgun to find the

number of the pizzeria he recommended earlier and order two extra-large pies with all the trimmings. When we arrive home, we plop down on the couch and crack open a couple of cold beers to drink while we wait for our food to be delivered.

"Thanks again for adding me to your lease. I was so glad not to have to fuck around with apartment hunting on top of everything else," I say.

We've kept in touch ever since college, and as soon as Colin heard I was transferring, he offered me one of his spare bedrooms. Fully furnished, with very reasonable rent too. He's a stand-up guy—genuine, hardworking, down to earth, mellow. He isn't even mad that I got a starting spot when he's been a backup kicker for years.

"No problem, bro. I'm stoked to be roommates with you again. It'll be just like old times." Colin grins. "Except now I won't have to smell your godawful laundry. Or kick you out every time I want to get laid."

I chuckle. "You're remembering wrong. I was the one kicking *you* out all the time."

He punches me lightly on the shoulder. "Ah, fuck you, man. The point is, sharing a dorm room is one of the things I definitely don't miss about college."

"Got that right."

We're interrupted by a knock on the door. We collect our pizzas and set them on the coffee table. For a while, we focus on inhaling the food while it's still hot, washing down every few bites with swigs of beer. When only a couple of slices remain, Colin leans back with a satisfied burp.

"Damn, that hit the spot. I'm always starving after training." He sighs, then shoots me a sidelong glance. "So, back in Philly . . ."

"What about it?" I ask suspiciously. I don't like his hesitation.

"A few months ago, you mentioned you and Trista were engaged. But now you're living out here. So, what's going on with that?"

Dammit. I might as well get this shitty story over with as fast as I can. "The short version is Trista cheated on me, and I broke it off."

Colin winces. "Fuck, dude, that's terrible. Sorry I asked."

"Nah, I figured it would come up sooner or later."

I'm actually surprised he hasn't heard the rumors before now. It wasn't exactly a secret. That shit spread through the league pretty fast considering she cheated with a player from my team.

We drink in silence for a minute or two. But Colin is restless, clearly itching to say something.

Finally, I say, "Spit it out."

"So, who was she cheating with?" he blurts.

I grimace. "Another Ranger."

Colin's eyes go wide. "One of your own teammates fucked your fiancée? Holy shit. Backstabbing assholes, both of 'em."

"I think they'd been fucking since before we were engaged, but yeah. That's why I wanted to get the hell out of Philly. No way could I keep working with that guy."

He shakes his head in dismay. "I don't blame you . . . damn. I would've pounded him into paste as soon as we got out on the field together, and I'd end up suspended from a game." He sits forward. "How did you catch them? And what did she say? Did you confront the other g—"

"Can we just drop it?" I snap.

Colin blinks at the sudden interruption, then leans back on the couch, looking sheepish. "Sorry. Got carried away."

"It's cool. I just . . . I'm pretty done with thinking about that whole thing."

"I don't blame you." Colin takes another sip of his beer, searching for another topic. "So . . . how was it seeing Jane again?"

This topic isn't much of an improvement. At least I don't have to tell any more painful stories, since Colin had a front-row seat to our breakup in my freshman year.

"Like a kick in the balls." I sigh. "From the way she's acting, I think she still hates me. I mean, it's been ten years. If I can get over it, why can't she? What the fuck else does she want me to do here?"

He gives me a wry twist of his lips. "That sucks . . . but try not to worry too much about it. For Jane, the job always comes first. No matter how she feels about someone, she never treats them different from anybody else. So just act normal, and she'll do the same."

The corner of my mouth twitches. "Yeah, that sounds like Jane." Tough but fair, level-headed, disciplined, dedicated to her work. Those qualities were part of what drew me to her in the first place. It's funny to see how much she's turned out like her dad.

Colin shrugs. "I wish I had something more useful to say, but getting on with your life is the best I can do."

"It's not bad advice." I pick at the label on my bottle. "Just out of curiosity, is Jane, uh, seeing anyone?"

He scratches his chin in thought. "Not that I know of. Actually, I don't think I've ever even seen her with a guy . . . except for Alex, but I'm pretty sure they're just friends. They go out for nachos, stuff like that."

That's a far cry from how I acted when we broke up. I went on a bender all throughout college, girl after girl after girl. It took me six years to settle on Trista, and another three years to propose to her, thinking that I'd finally found my forever. Look how *that* brilliant fucking idea turned out.

Out of nowhere, Colin asks, "Are you really over her?"

I give him a bewildered look. "Who, Trista? Of course. She—"

"No, stupid. I meant Jane."

I almost have to laugh. The truth is you don't ever really get over a woman like Jane. For me, she'll always be The One Who Got Away.

But what I say is, "Absolutely. I came here to win, nothing else. I intend to play the best football of my goddamn life, and if I'm gonna do that, I have to put all my focus on the game. I don't have time for any distractions."

No matter how gorgeous that distraction might be. This team and this city are supposed to be my fresh start, and I'll be damned if I blow this second chance.

"Fuck yeah." Colin laughs, slapping me on the shoulder. "That's the spirit. Rack up some nice big Hawk victories for us."

"You can bet on it." I stand up. "Speaking of which, I should probably start getting ready for bed."

He squints at the clock in confusion. "Already? It's not even nine yet. I was just about to ask if you wanted to fire up the Xbox."

"Didn't I just tell you I was going to eat, sleep, and breathe football from now on?" I give him a raised-eyebrow smirk. “And I’m not the only one who has to be on the practice field at the crack of dawn, y’know.”

Colin groans. “Don’t remind me. Fine, I’ll kick your ass some other time.”

I snort at him and head off to brush my teeth, half of me hoping I won’t see Jane tomorrow . . . and the other half unable to stop wondering if she’ll be watching me train.

CHAPTER *Three*

Jane

If someone had told me a week ago that it was going to be difficult for me to hate Weston Chase, I would have laughed that person out of my office. I have a well-stocked arsenal of material that gave me every reason to believe that I would have no trouble giving this asshole the cold shoulder for the entire season. And I was ready to do just that.

The problem is, my ten-year-old evidence of Wes's douchebaggery just isn't holding up to the player I see at practice every day.

He's always the first one at the training facility in the morning, sometimes even before my dad, and he's consistently the last to hit the showers. And it's not just a sometimes thing. It's an every-single-practice thing. He's made an admirable effort—I'll give him that.

"Chase!" Dad barks. "You better not be throwing like that at the Philly game! We're not ending on that note. Run it again!"

We're almost at the end of the longest practice we've had all week, and for a lot of the players, it shows. One by one, they're getting burnt out, dropping more and more F-bombs each time Dad calls for another run of a play.

Except for Wes.

Obviously, he's getting pretty worn out. His throw isn't looking as good as it did first thing this morning when practice started. But mentally, he's still 100 percent in it. I've never seen a player this driven, this passionate about improving.

The receivers bitch to the coaches and toss a little friendly trash talk Wes's way for his lousy throw, but Wes doesn't say a word. He just adjusts his helmet and runs back to the line, prepping to restart the play.

The high-pitched screech of Dad's whistle pierces the air, and this time, Wes throws a flawless spiral right into the hands of a wide receiver. Perfection.

And perfection is exactly what the coaches are expecting with our first away game coming up. Two days from now, we'll be landing in Philly to play the Rangers, a game that every sports blogger in the country has been ramping up since we signed Wes last week.

The rivalry between the Hawks and the Rangers is already one of the most famous in the league, but with rumors flying all over social media as to why Wes left the Rangers at the last minute, the buildup to his first game against his old team has been insane.

I've seen how that kind of media coverage has affected players before, making them quick to snap at the coach or just completely shut down, refusing to take direction or run drills. But not Wes. Somehow, he works harder and harder at every practice.

"Attaboy, Chase! All right, guys, huddle up, huddle up!"

As the players and assistant coaches circle to wrap up practice, I desperately fight my instincts to check out Wes's butt in those skintight football pants. Did I leave my self-control at home this morning? Or is it that sitting in the bleachers and watching Wes play puts me right back in girlfriend mode?

Either way, I'd better slip out of here before the players do to avoid any possible run-ins. I stuff the playbook and my water bottle into my laptop bag and sling it over my shoulder, standing up and eyeing the exit just as the players start to disperse.

"Yo, Jane! Wait up!"

Alex's deep voice interrupts my clean getaway. He's jogging my way with his helmet in his hands, his dark hair plastered to his forehead with sweat.

I scan the field and see that Wes is at a safe distance, talking with one of the assistant coaches. I can hang around for a minute or two and still be in the clear.

"Work up enough of a sweat today?" I tease, and he shakes his wet hair like a dog, making me recoil to stay out of the splash zone. "You need a shower ASAP. What do you want?"

He grabs a seat on the bleachers, but I make a point of remaining standing. I can't hang around long with Wes only a few hundred feet away.

Alex obviously senses my discomfort, because he cuts right to the chase. "What are you doing tonight?"

"Probably working, followed by a wild night

of watching home-renovation shows and falling asleep early on the couch," I say with a shrug. "Why, what's up?"

"The team is getting together around seven for dinner. Just a super-casual thing. You're coming, right?"

My gaze flicks to Wes. "The whole team?"

Alex rolls his eyes. "Yes, Jane. The whole team. And you. It's at Colin's house. C'mon, you never miss a team dinner."

"Yeah, but I . . . I'm really tired, Alex. I haven't even started packing for Philly yet. And I don't want to interfere with team bonding, especially since we just brought on a new player." I'm stringing together any excuse my brain can come up with. Maybe I can fake a phone call with Mr. Flores and pretend he's asking me to work all night.

"Look, Jane. You don't have to bullshit me," Alex says flatly. "Your dad already told me about your history with the new guy."

"He *what*?" I snap, a little louder than I'd like. I pretend not to notice that a few lingering second-string guys are looking over to see what I'm overreacting about. "He shouldn't have told you that," I say in a much lower, calmer voice, flashing my best *everything is fine, please don't look at me* smile at the nosy players.

"I think it's cool that he wanted your closest friend on the team to know what was going on with you," Alex says. "Plus, you were acting weird as hell around Wes, anyway. I would've figured it out on my own eventually. I know you pretty well. And I know he's the reason you're trying to skip out on dinner."

"Fine. I don't want to see him. Is that a crime?"

"Come on, Jane. He's just one player. There's a whole team of other guys who want to see you there." When that doesn't work, he gives me a stupid pouty look like a two-year-old who isn't getting his way. "Pleeeease? For me?"

I roll my eyes. "Fine. But only so you'll stop bugging me, and I don't have to smell you any longer." I wave my hand in front of my nose dramatically, which makes him laugh.

"I promise I'll smell much better tonight. I'll text you Colin's address, okay?" He jumps to his feet and slugs me in the arm before jogging off to the locker room.

I check my watch—it's already after noon, and I have work to do before this dinner. Now I really do have to book it out of here in a hurry. I dismiss the thought of trying to get work done from home, knowing that if I go back to my place, I'll spend every minute I have picking out the perfect *I tried, but not too hard* outfit for tonight.

I've got to be in my office if I have a prayer of getting anything done, so I head upstairs, log in to my computer, and refer to my ever-growing to-do list. If I can just get a few details worked out for the upcoming Philly trip, I'll feel a whole lot better about taking the rest of the evening off.

Unfortunately, there are a lot more than a few details to take care of. My in-box has at least twenty emails from staffers asking about details and assignments in preparation for our first away game. Time to crack my knuckles, put my earbuds in, and get down to business.

I start responding to my first email, but I hardly get three words in before my mind wanders to what Alex said about me acting "weird as hell" around Wes. Did all the guys on the team notice that, or was that something only Alex picked up on because he knows me so well?

I thought I had been doing a pretty decent job of acting professional, all things considered, but my actual interaction with Wes has pretty much been limited to accidentally hitting him with the door to the locker room after his press conference.

Avoiding him at practice is easy enough. With his helmet on, the risk of making eye contact is low. And thank God it is, because those night-sky-colored blue eyes of his are hypnotizing. Not that it matters. No amount of hypnosis could make me forget what he did to me.

My phone buzzes and pulls me out of my head. It's Alex, texting me the address for tonight, along with a message that says, *See you tonight!*

• • •

The second I walk through Colin's front door, I'm greeted with the smell of men's deodorant and pizza grease, the official smell of any Hawks gathering. Somebody should really talk to the marketing team about making a cologne. I'm sure there are plenty of fans out there crazy enough to buy it.

"Hey, you made it!" Alex calls out, rising from his seat on one of the many couches in the enormous living room, which is filled to the brim with guys.

Colin has a big house, but these are big dudes, so couches that are made to sit three or four people can only comfortably fit two players. Somebody else hops up from the floor and steals Alex's seat right away, yelling, "He didn't call seat check!"

One of the second-string guys passes me a paper plate and points me in the direction of the kitchen as Alex pulls me into a side hug.

"You hungry?" he asks, as if he doesn't already know the answer.

"Take me to the pizza," I say, eager to get out of this room full of guys. I know Wes is somewhere in that mess of muscular dudes, but I don't want to look for him. I'd rather just stick by Alex's side and trust that he won't steer me wrong.

There isn't a flat surface in the kitchen that isn't covered by a pizza box. Nobody can eat quite like a pro football team. As I load up my plate with two slices of mushroom pizza, Alex grabs a whole box for himself. I love working with football players. They never make me feel like I'm eating too much.

"Is there anywhere we can sit?" I ask, hoping *that's far away from Weston Chase* is implied.

"I'm sure I can chase a few second-stringers off a couch," Alex says, surveying the living room for his target.

I giggle, but my face immediately falls when I see Wes heading toward the kitchen to get seconds.

"Um, I'm going to use the bathroom," I say quickly, handing my plate to Alex.

He gives me a knowing look but takes my plate from me. "Upstairs," he says, nodding at the staircase.

I dash off, taking the steps two at a time. After I give myself a quick pep talk in the mirror, I'm sure I'll be all set to handle the rest of the night.

The second floor of this house is just as big as the downstairs, so I get to work opening and closing doors in an attempt to identify which one is the bathroom. Unfortunately, before I can find it, someone else finds me.

"Hey, Jane."

I freeze, my hand on the doorknob of yet another room that isn't the bathroom. I'd know that deep voice anywhere. "Weston."

I spin around. Sure enough, there he is, all six foot three of him. My breath quivers in my lungs as I look for an escape route, but he has me cornered.

"Can we talk? Clear the air so this isn't so damn uncomfortable?" His voice is so rich and deep, yet soft at the same time. It hasn't changed at all, and I hate that it still affects me.

I'm praying someone else will come up the stairs and give me an out from this conversation, but there's nobody. Just Wes and me. I can feel my face turning red, either in anger or anxiety, I don't know.

The thing is, I can't do this right now. I can't lash out at him in somebody else's house with the whole team downstairs. I'm nothing if not professional, and I've never given this team a reason to doubt that.

"I have nothing to say to you," I finally manage to say.

He does that little snort-laugh that I used to think was so cute, but now it feels like a punch in the gut.

"So you're still not over me. Is that what this is about?"

Now it's my turn to laugh. "Get over yourself, Wes. If you think for even a second that I'm still pining for you after all this time, then you should get your ego in check. I have zero interest in even seeing you. The only reason I'm at this team dinner is for Alex."

"Oh, so you're fucking him now?" Wes blurts, his nostrils flaring. "Guess you were always into football players, weren't you?"

"You don't know me, Weston. You don't know me at all anymore, and you have zero right to know who I'm *fucking*, as you so eloquently put it. You were the last player I ever dated, and I can promise you I'll never make that mistake again. Now, do you want to keep making wrong guesses about who I am and what I do with my life, or can I go now?"

I give him half a second to answer before walking away. He steps to the side, thank God, and lets me past him. He's done with me, for now.

Alex is waiting at the bottom of the stairs, and by the look on his face, he heard every word. "You want to go outside for a second?"

I nod furiously, clenching my jaw to keep from screaming. We step out onto the back deck, and I release the longest breath of my life, letting my balled-up hands unfurl.

"I am so, so sorry, Jane," he says, staring down at me and rubbing the back of his neck with one hand. "I shouldn't have made you come tonight. I really didn't know things were that dicey between you two."

"They're not," I say, running my fingers nervously through my hair. "I just lost my temper, I guess. I don't know. I'm sorry too."

We stand there in the silence for a second, which feels nice compared to what I just went through. Eventually, he squeezes my shoulder in a gesture meant to comfort. My face feels like it's faded from bright red back to its normal color, and my breath is evening out.

"Are you going to be all right?" he asks, and not just out of courtesy. By the way Alex says it, I can tell he honestly isn't sure. Frankly, I'm not really sure either. But I also don't have a choice.

"I'm fine," I say on an exhale. "I can handle it."

Or at least, that's what I have to keep telling myself.

CHAPTER *Four*

Weston

Jane leaves the party soon after we blew up at each other. I don't even have to search or ask anyone to know; I can just tell she's gone.

I wander around restlessly through the dense sea of laughing, chatting players. I don't feel like eating or drinking anymore, but just to have something to do, I grab a fresh beer and go sit on the couch.

Suddenly, loud rock music blasts through the house. Someone must have found Colin's stereo. One guy whistles loudly, and a chorus of others join in with hollers and whoops. The party turns more upbeat around me as I sit alone, nursing my beer and the bitter taste Jane left in my mouth.

A woman plops down beside me. "Hi, Wes,"

she coos. "You having a good time?"

I glance at her. She doesn't ring any bells. Young, maybe early twenties. Her body is scrupulously taut and tanned. Her tight pink crop top and microscopic denim shorts expose a bellybutton ring surrounded by miles of midriff. On the other side of the room, a similarly dressed woman is talking to one of our defensemen. He's grinning and puffed up, and she's giggling, cocking her head in a cutesy way, touching his arm.

So they're jersey chasers. That explains why a total stranger knew my name. Every major team has a gaggle of groupie girls who follow them around like lost puppies. Still, how did they even find this party? Tonight was supposed to be a private team dinner.

"Just fine," I grunt out.

She either doesn't hear or ignores my grouchy tone. "I'm Jess. It's so great to meet you—I'm such a huge Hawks fan. I watch all your games." Starry-eyed, she scoots closer.

Ironic that she's trying to chat me up when I haven't even played a game as part of this team yet. But for some girls, all it takes is that "QB" after my name to send their panties flying.

"Thanks for your support," I say, like some kind of canned publicity statement.

She practically shoves her cleavage against my shoulder. "I'd love to hear some good football stories. But it's kinda hard to hear in here. Want to find somewhere . . . quieter?"

Normally, I'd at least consider taking her up on it. I don't go out of my way to score, but if a good-looking woman comes to me with an offer, why not?

But for some reason, the idea is totally unappealing. Worse than unappealing.

"Hello? I said—"

I get up so quickly, she almost falls over. "Sorry," I mutter. Even I can tell I sound unconvincing. "I'm not interested."

"Fine, jeez." She flounces off in a huff, probably to try her luck with another player.

That was rude of me, but I can't bring myself to care too much. I can't take one more second of this noise, this crowd. I don't know why I feel so awful.

I dump the rest of my beer in the sink and retreat to my bedroom. I lock the door, lie down on my bed, and shove earplugs in my ears to block out the chaos still raging downstairs.

But sleep won't come. I roll onto my back and stare at the ceiling.

Jane and I used to lie like this all the time on the grassy hill behind our high school. Not saying much, just holding hands, warmed by the sun and each other's closeness. She'd look over at me with a soft, beautifully peaceful smile, and I'd be lost forever.

God, she once filled my whole world. It was so long ago, it should be strange to think about, but the memories are so crystal clear, they make me ache. We were each other's first crush, first kiss, first everything. We'd planned on being each other's last too . . . until I screwed it all up like the dumbass kid I was.

I was just too young. I know that now. I let my newfound college freedoms and pressures get the better of me. Wiser now, I wouldn't make the same mistakes twice. But there would never be a "twice."

That one chance was all I got, and understanding how it went wrong doesn't make my regrets sting any less.

• • •

Even though our flight to Philadelphia isn't until two in the afternoon, half the players are still bitching about their hangovers. As soon as the seat-belt sign turns off with a ding, my phone lights up with a message from Colin.

U ready to wreck the rangers, bro?

Hell yes, I type back.

A lot of people have been asking me if I feel conflicted about playing my first game for the Hawks against my old team, but even though I mostly got along great with my fellow Rangers, Philly holds too many bad memories to feel sentimental about. And right now, I've got something way more pressing on my mind.

From my seat far in the rear of the plane, I can just barely see the back of Jane's head if I lean forward. The uncomfortable knot in my chest grows every time I catch a glimpse of her.

I really should apologize for cornering her last night. Hell, I *want* to apologize, which doesn't happen very often. But somehow, I just can't make myself stand up and get my ass over there. We're surrounded by Hawks players and staff. Talking to her now would air our dirty laundry in front of everyone we work with. I'd never hear the end of it.

Berating myself for being a coward as well as a douchebag, I decide to apologize the instant I can get her alone . . . which, let's be real, probably won't happen anytime soon, given how determinedly she's been avoiding me.

In the meantime, I need to stop driving myself nuts. I deliberately tear my gaze from Jane and look around. The guys seated to my left and right are tapping away on their phones . . . on Tinder, to be exact.

My lip curls. Seriously, already? They can't even wait two hours until we touch down to try to set up their next conquests in Philly? And while it's harder to tell what the guy across the aisle is doing, what little I can see looks a lot like the same thing.

The sight sours my mood even further. I've witnessed all kinds of messed-up shit on the road. Guys treating away games like marathon frat parties, getting so wasted they could barely play the next morning, chasing hookups whether they were single or not. I even had a teammate once who had a wife at home and a girlfriend in another city.

The whole thing is sickening. We're here to

win the goddamn game and that's it, not run around on pussy patrol. And we're definitely not here to break hearts.

I pull up our playbook on my phone and review our strategy for the umpteenth time, just so I don't have to look at what my teammates or Jane or anyone else is doing.

It's well after dark by the time we're all checked in and settled at our hotel. Colin waves our room's welcome packet in my face.

"Where do you want to get dinner?"

"I dunno. This place has its own restaurant, doesn't it?" Most of the Hawks have wandered off to find food, and probably girls, but I actually care about keeping curfew and getting a decent night's sleep before our game.

Colin shrugs. "Sure. I don't give a crap so long as I get some food ASAP."

We head downstairs, get a table, and order a feast. I've almost polished off my roast chicken and fries when Alex walks up to us wearing a dark scowl. Alexei "Alex" Ivan isn't someone you want to fuck around with. He's easily six foot four, and his reputation as a badass linebacker is well-deserved.

"I want to talk to you, Chase," he growls.

I take my time chewing and swallowing before I reply with a terse, "Yeah?"

Maybe he's not sleeping with Jane, like Colin said, but I still don't have to be gleeful about the fact that he gets to hang out with her while I get jack shit. Especially not with that obnoxious look on his face that makes it clear he's here to pick a fight.

Alex crosses his beefy arms over his chest, as if he can intimidate me with his size, when I know I could take him if it came down to it. "Jane was about ready to lose her shit last night. What the hell is wrong with you? Where do you get off talking to her like that? Who do you think you are?"

"Dude, chill," Colin says.

But Alex just shakes his head. "This isn't about you. It's about this prick right here."

I lower my voice. "You might want to back off."

"No, I don't think I do. I think I want to take you outside and beat the hell out of you."

"I get it, okay?" I snap. "I fucked up royally. Not that it's any of your business."

"Of course it's my business, asshole! She's my friend, and I won't let y—" The way Alex does a double-take and stares at me is almost funny. "Wait . . . what? You admit it?"

"Yeah. The rest is between me and her, so quit riding my ass."

Alex throws his hands in the air. "Whatever, man. As long as you make it up to her."

"I will as soon as you fuck off and let me finish my dinner."

Alex flips me the bird as he goes, but at least he leaves.

Colin lets out a baffled laugh. "Well, that sure was something."

"No kidding." I raise my fork to my lips, then stop again when I hear a commotion from the lobby. "Oh, for fuck's sake. What now?"

"It's probably nothing," Colin mumbles through a mouthful of his cheesesteak sandwich.

Maybe so, but Jane is in the mix, and I can never stay uninvolved when it comes to her.

I stand up. "I think I'm done eating anyway. I'm going to go check it out."

Colin grunts in acknowledgment and swallows. "Does that mean I can have the rest of your fries?"

"Knock yourself out," I say over my shoulder as I make a beeline to the lobby.

Jane and two players are blocking the elevator. One of them, who I recognize as our fullback, Woodruff, is in the middle of an enthusiastic explanation, arms waving and everything.

"I could've sworn I packed them, but they're just *gone*, and I should've been in bed half an hour ago, and—"

The other one, a cornerback named Ramirez, interjects. "Seriously, he's got to get at least ten hours of sleep or he's gonna play like shit."

Woodruff frowns at him. "Shut up, man."

Jane holds up her hand with a weary expression. "Guys, please relax. I'll go out and buy some right now, and you can go on to bed. Everything is going to be fine."

"What's going on?" I say as I catch up to them.

"My lucky socks," Woodruff almost yells. "The left one has to be black and the right one has to be orange. I don't know what the fuck happened to the pair I usually bring."

I hold back a snort. Lots of football players are superstitious about that sort of thing. I really shouldn't laugh at his pain, but it's hard not to see the humor in a grown-ass man hollering about socks in the middle of a hotel lobby.

"Which is why I'm going to run to the store right now and buy replacements as soon as everyone lets me get out of here." Jane gives the two players a pointed look, placing her hands on her slim hips.

"I'll come with you," I say. It's late, after all, and I know from years of living here that Philly isn't the world's safest city.

Her expression frosts over the instant she looks at me.

I don't like what I glimpse in her eyes . . . she's not wary, exactly, but her guard is up, as if she's expecting to have to dodge unpleasantness. The thought that I'm hurting her just by being around her settles as a bitter lump in the pit of my stomach.

I glance back at Colin sitting in the hotel restaurant. Maybe I should ask him to go with her instead. I'm not wild about that idea, but at least she'd be protected.

"Fine, whatever," she says.

I blink at her. "Really?"

"Come if you want. I don't care." She turns on her heel and heads into the hall.

I join her in the elevator just before the doors close. I follow her through the lobby and the parking lot to the team's black minivan.

"Good thing Mr. Flores always rents us a car during away games," I say, trying to break the ice.

"He likes to be prepared for emergencies," Jane says, as deadpan as if she's reading from an employee manual.

"Emergencies like lucky socks?" I joke.

She doesn't reply, just fishes the keys out of her pocket. "Here, I know you always want to drive. I can navigate."

Does she know me? It's been ten years. She's right, though. I do still prefer being in the driver's seat.

"Sure, thanks." I hold out my hand.

She drops the keys into it, not touching me.

We get in, and I pull out of the lot while she pokes at her phone, trying to find somewhere to buy socks at nine thirty in the goddamn evening.

For a long time, we roll along the Philadelphia streets in silence, broken only by Jane occasionally giving me terse directions.

I can't help but remember the last time I drove her around like this. The summer after I graduated from high school, before everything fell apart . . .

Jane beside me, windows rolled down, her amber hair whipping around in the warm breeze, her smile glowing brighter than the August sun. Us together, laughing, stealing kisses, murmuring sweet nothings, making foolish teenage plans for the blissful future we were so sure lay ahead of us.

This atmosphere couldn't be more different now. It's as tense and painful as a cramped muscle.

I try to break the ice with the first question that pops into my head. "So, uh, how long have you been working for the Hawks?"

She doesn't even glance up from her phone. "Since college."

"Do you like Mr. Flores? Is he a good manager?"

"Mm-hmm."

"How's . . . uh . . ." I rack my brain for a way to finish that sentence.

Being friends with Alex? She'll think I'm trying to revive our fight.

Working with your dad? No, that'll seem like a dig too, like I'm insinuating she inherited her job instead of earning it. And I know what working with Ken Royce is like just as well as Jane does. Not only is he my boss now, he was practically a father to me growing up—he got me into football, taught me how to throw a perfect spiral, listened to all the teenage problems my real dad didn't stick around to hear.

She says nothing, letting me flounder.

Fuck it. "Seen any good movies lately?"

"No."

She's clearly determined not to give me anything more than driving directions. I give up on small talk for now and just drive.

Jane stares out the passenger side window. Occasionally, she glances at me, but whenever I look back, she hurriedly turns away again.

This is ridiculous. We can't go on like this. We can't work together if we can barely talk. And not that I'd ever tell anyone, but the constant awareness that she's upset makes my chest tight.

No more procrastinating . . . I need to smooth things over. Several times, I open my mouth to start, only to stall out at the last second.

God, why is this so hard?

"Listen," I finally blurt.

Jane looks at me. "What?"

Well, I can't back out now. I have to finish what I've started.

I stare straight ahead at the road as I mutter, "At the, uh, party last night . . . I shouldn't have accused you of fucking Alex."

Her eyes widen slightly. But she doesn't speak, just watches me. Maybe she's trying to figure out if my apology is sincere. I don't know. The only thing that's clear is she's waiting for me to finish talking.

"What I mean is . . ." I rake my hand through my hair. "Whether you've fucked him or not doesn't matter. You can fuck or not fuck whoever you want. It's none of my business anymore." *Stop saying* fuck, *you idiot.* I clamp my lips shut.

For a moment, she just blinks at me. "Thanks?" she says, sounding confused and still very much unimpressed. "I'm so glad I have your permission.

I'll keep that in mind next time I'm making bedroom-related decisions."

"Dammit, don't be like that. I'm trying to apologize, and you're just crapping all over it," I snap before I can get a hold of myself.

Her lips press into a tight line. She scoffs low and angry in her throat. "Then maybe figure out a better apology."

I fight down the angry retort boiling on the back of my tongue and force myself to just breathe for a minute before we get into another knock-down, drag-out fight.

The thought of anybody else in Jane's bedroom feels like a knife in my gut, but that's not her problem to solve. I need to suck it up and get over it. Her life is her own . . . and I'm not part of it. That ended a long time ago.

I grind my teeth. "What I should've said is just, I'm sorry. I went up to talk to you because I wanted shit to be less awkward at work, and then I ended up yelling at you and making everything even more awkward. I made it all about me and got personal when I should've stayed professional. I promise to try not to act like such a dickhead from now on."

She blinks at me. It's hard to see details clearly

in the alternating bars of shadow and dim streetlight, especially while I'm trying to watch the road at the same time. But I think I see her expression soften.

Finally, she says quietly, "Thank you." She twirls her hair around her finger. "I, uh, wasn't exactly using my indoor voice either."

I shrug. "I wouldn't have kept my cool if someone had said that stuff to me."

She hums, sounding mollified. My shoulders slowly start to unknot as we drive on. Maybe things between us still aren't great, but the atmosphere in the car has definitely lightened.

She reaches for the radio dial and turns on a rap song that was popular when we were in high school. I can't help the smile that overtakes my face. It feels like a sign.

Jane reaches for the radio again, but I stop her.

"Leave it."

"Yeah?" she asks, her voice unsure.

"Yeah. Haven't heard this in forever."

She settles back in her seat, her slender fingers drumming out the beat on her thigh.

“You used to love this song, right?” I ask.

Jane flashes me that pretty smile of hers I used to love, but this time, it’s more guarded than I remember.

“Still do.”

CHAPTER *Five*

Jane

It's ten years later and I'm back where it all started—with me sitting in Weston Chase's passenger's seat.

Granted, it's a rental van now, not the old blue pickup truck he used to drive, the one I could hear rumbling from two blocks away when he came to pick me up for Saturday-night dates. We had our first kiss in that truck, and a few other firsts too, since getting privacy with our parents always around was next to impossible.

For four years, I sat shotgun while he drove, and now we're back in the very same position. Different car, same shit. It almost feels like old times.

The familiarity is sweet. He has all the same quirks, like the way he triple-checks that I have my seat belt on, and how he drums the steering wheel with his thumbs at red lights. It's crazy how little he's changed in some ways, especially with how much he's changed physically.

He was far from scrappy in high school—he was still a football player, after all—but he definitely has to shift the seat a lot farther back now to make room for all of him. Six foot three and two hundred fifteen pounds of pure, unadulterated muscle. Any other guy that built would intimidate the crap out of me, yet I don't feel that way with Wes at all.

Even when he had me cornered outside the bathroom at Colin's house, I wasn't afraid of him. Angry, yes, but never intimidated. But now I have an apology for that. That's another way he's changed. In high school, Wes never would have apologized the way he did tonight. He used to be so stubborn. I guess he really has grown up in more ways than one.

A thousand forbidden memories flood my mind at once. Sweet kisses and whispered promises. And something more specific lodges itself in my brain, unreeling like a forgotten film. Weston balancing on his forearms above me while I lay spread out in his bed. With his mom working late that particular

July night, we dared to undress each other completely, lounging in bed together, taking our time. It was much different from our hurried encounters in his truck.

Wes's lips met mine, his tongue invading my mouth, and I eagerly kissed him back. I was so eager for it all. And when his hands moved to the clasp of my bra, I lifted off the mattress, allowing him to remove the last stitch of clothing between us. His gaze tracked hotly down my body.

"Fuck . . ." His tone was reverent and sent my pulse skittering. "You're perfect."

One rough palm caressed my breast, and I let out a groan.

"I can't *not* touch these." He grinned.

"Yes. Touch me."

After that, it was game over. He worshiped my body from head to toe, kissing and sucking on my breasts until I was writhing beneath him. Then he spent a long time between my legs, learning what I liked, how to touch me, how to make me come against his hand, and then his mouth.

He was so eager, and I was happy to let him learn. He elicited responses from my body I didn't even know I had, found places that made me whimper and call out his name. Nibbling on my inner thighs, then sucking my clit, petting it with his tongue. Calloused fingers massaging my breasts, finding sensitive spots on my wrists. My neck exploited with soft, sucking kisses that made me moan.

I know that teenage boys aren't known for their sexual prowess, and Wes wasn't perfect, but he was enthusiastic about pleasing me, and that made all the difference.

When he finally rolled on a condom, I'd already come twice and was so wet and ready, I pulled him closer. And then the broad head of him penetrated me for the first time while his lips stayed glued to mine. It hurt, but not as bad as I expected it to, and Wes let out the most delicious-sounding groan in the world.

Burying his soft-stubbled cheek against my neck, he took a deep, stuttering breath, stilling inside me. "Don't fucking move. I want to make this last."

But those words were futile, because after an hour of foreplay and then only a half dozen thrusts of his hips, he groaned out his release, filling the condom.

We laughed together after that, me teasing him, and him promising me a better performance next time. But the truth was, I didn't care one bit that my first sexual encounter lasted all of forty-five seconds. I felt cherished and beautiful and completely loved from my head to my toes.

"You okay over there?" he asks, drawing me from my thoughts.

I draw a shaky inhale and nod.

As we're waiting for the light to change, Wes fusses with the radio for a bit, changing it from a commercial until he lands on a station that's playing more old-school hip hop.

"You still into rap?" he asks, then snickers when he sees I'm already mouthing the lyrics along with the beat. "I'll take that as a yes."

"GPS says we'll be there in five minutes," I say, referring to the directions to the nearest Walmart that I've got pulled up on my phone.

"Perfect. Long enough for the song to change so you can prove it's not a fluke that you know all the words to this one."

I gladly accept his challenge. When the next song comes on, I don't just mouth the lyrics, I rap along. It's something I usually only do when I'm in the car by myself, but I feel so totally comfortable that I just go for it.

Wes hums along to the parts he knows, soaking in my performance, just like he used to do way back when. It all feels so easy, so natural.

We pull into the parking lot just as the song ends.

"All right, let's find some damn socks," Wes says as he pulls the key from the ignition.

I grab a basket on the way into the store, half by instinct and half because I'm notorious for leaving big-box stores like this with a dozen things I don't need. The layout here is different from our Walmart at home, and a quick once-over of the place offers me zero clues as to where we're going to find these socks.

"Maybe we should ask someone," I say, but Wes immediately shoots that idea down.

"We don't need help. I can find it," he says gruffly.

I roll my eyes. *Men.*

It doesn't take long before we're totally lost, wandering aimlessly through the dairy aisle in pursuit of the menswear section.

"Remember how you used to dip Doritos in cream cheese?" I giggle, picking up a family-size tub.

Wes stops dead in his tracks and swivels his head toward me, his brow scrunched down. "Uh, what do you mean, *used to*?"

I nearly drop the cream cheese in surprise. "You're joking, right? You don't still eat that grossness."

Wes's toned forearms ripple as he crosses his arms over his chest, taking a power stance. "Come on. I can't have one guilty pleasure?"

"You are *so* disgusting!" I roll my eyes, tossing the tub of cream cheese into my basket and making a mental note to grab a few bags of Doritos before we leave. Without any sense of direction in here, I'm sure we'll end up in the chip aisle before long.

After a few more laps around the store, my basket is filled with anything but socks. Two big bags of Doritos for Wes, a box of my favorite oatmeal cream cookies, and a six-pack of beer that Wes claims is "just in case."

We finally find our way to our target destination—the completely unorganized racks of men's socks. Splitting up for the sake of time, each of us takes a rack in a race to find the socks that fit the description we were given. Wes wins, emerging with two pairs in the right size, one in black and one in neon orange.

"Might as well buy both," I say, and Wes tosses both pairs into our basket.

After we check out, he insists on carrying the bags back to the car. I guess he's learned a bit more chivalry in the ten years we've been apart.

The radio starts up playing a wild dance beat as Wes turns the key in the ignition. I would recognize this intro beat anywhere. It's a classic from our high school days. I remember dancing to this song at prom, and making out in Wes's truck with this beat playing through his old busted speakers.

"No way. I can't believe they're still playing this song on the radio. It's practically ancient," I say with a laugh.

Wes turns up the dial. We both know the words, so it looks like this one will be a duet. Neither of us is exactly an undiscovered singing sensation, but that doesn't stop us from belting out the chorus at the top of our lungs.

Halfway through the second verse, I realize that this whole evening, I've totally forgotten to hate Wes. I don't want to admit it, but I actually had a really good time with him. Somehow, he turned a stupid run to Walmart for a pair of athletic socks into a really fun night.

As the song dies down and the radio DJ's voice blares through the speakers, Wes shuts the radio off. "We're ending on a high note," he says. "No song is going to top that performance."

We ride in comfortable silence for the last minute back to the hotel. Our lucky-sock rescue mission complete, we strut victoriously into the lobby, which is completely empty. Normally, there would be players still running around, chatting up jersey chasers at the hotel bar.

I check my watch. Shit, it's already eleven? We're way past curfew, but this was totally worth it.

We slink through the lobby to the elevator, my fingers ultra-crossed that no coaches see us, especially my dad. Now this really feels like high school. Luckily, we make it into the elevator completely unnoticed.

"Do you want to come over to my room for

some snacks? I can't eat all these Doritos myself," Wes says as we step off the elevator and onto our floor. He pauses for a second to laugh at himself. "Well, actually I can," he admits, "but I'm cool with sharing."

I admit I'm tempted by the offer, more so because of Wes than because of the Doritos, but somehow, being in his room with him seems like a bad idea. I said I'd stay far away from him, and that doesn't involve alone time behind a locked hotel room door.

"It's already past eleven." I tap the face of my watch for emphasis. "That's past team curfew, and we're going to be exhausted tomorrow. We'd both better play it safe and get some shut-eye."

Wes nods, then reaches into the bag and hands my oatmeal cream cookies to me. "I'll get this special delivery to Brad. No way has that moron fallen asleep while he's still stressing about his lucky socks."

I smirk. "Thanks. Have a good night, Wes."

"You too. Thanks for letting me come with you."

I feel like I'm the one who owes him a thank-you. Thank you for such a fun evening; thank you for not being the douchebag I thought you were. But it's late, and I'm too tired for that conversation.

My keycard unlocks my room with a soft click, and with a gentle wave of my fingers, I slip behind the door, then watch Wes walk away through the peephole.

Maybe this season won't be so bad after all.

CHAPTER Six

Weston

The horn blares for a time-out, and everyone on the field skids to a halt. I hear several of my teammates swear, and at least one of them spikes their helmet into the turf. I'm pretty tempted to do the same.

Fourth quarter has ended . . . and the score is still tied. Which forces us into overtime.

I take off my helmet and look over at Jane, sitting in the first row of the press box reserved for media, PR, and important people connected to the team. The disbelief and gnawing worry on her face reflects my own.

I grind my teeth. How the fuck did this happen? Analysts favored the Hawks to win easily against the Rangers, but they came after us with a vengeance. Somehow, we ended up in a dead heat.

The ref motions to us for the coin toss. Alex, our defensive captain, and Luke, the special-teams captain, join me on the walk to the fifty-yard line. I stare stonily into the Rangers' captains' eyes, not letting my tightly wound nerves show. It's all come down to one last play. Anything could happen . . . but I vow not to let it.

I've been thinking about pivotal moments like this one since I was eight years old and first learning the game, sitting starry-eyed in front of the TV, cheering my idols to victory and fantasizing about one day standing among their ranks. I should be used to it by now.

I've been playing professional football for six years. I've thrown thousands of passes, run hundreds of plays, won more games than I can count. But every time always feels brand new, because I'm always competing with myself to up my game. Working my ass off to train harder, run faster, throw farther, set new records just to smash through them later. It's a rush like no other. An addiction. A dream come true.

"Visitor calls," the ref says.

"Heads," I say.

The ref flips the coin into the air, catches it, and reveals heads. "Hawks take possession."

Letting out a long exhale, I turn to confer briefly with Alex and Luke, then tell the ref, "We'll receive."

The ref points to the Rangers' special-teams captain. "Then you'll kick."

Ignoring the captain's poisonous glare, I turn and walk back to the visitors' side. I need this to go one way—our way.

All game long, I've been trying to tell myself that this is any other game, that I'll play hard and win because it's what I do. Only the truth is, it's not just any game. This is my first time playing against this team since I was traded to the Hawks. My first time back on this field since I caught my fiancée cheating with a teammate. Fittingly, number sixty-nine.

As the Hawks circle for our final huddle, I push all other thoughts out of my head. This might be a personal vendetta for me, but the only thing that matters is winning. We've been playing hard for hours, but we can't afford to be tense and tired now. We need to play smart and make the best possible use of the other team's exhaustion.

I bring my hands together in a decisive clap. "I played with the Rangers for years. I know how these guys operate, their strengths and weaknesses. If we let them, they'll drag this out for as long as humanly possible, just to wear us down."

Alex eyes me. "You better know what you're doing."

"As long as you and your guys are there to ram the living shit out of anyone who so much as looks at the ball."

That gets a chuckle out of him. "Why the hell am I letting you talk me into this?"

Taking that as agreement, I quickly outline a strategy that makes Luke smile in approval. Even Alex is reluctantly nodding.

Then we go to work—perfectly executing that plan until somehow, the ball is squeezing past their men and into the end zone.

Everyone freezes. A hush falls over the crowd as the two refs confer by the goalposts. Then one of them raises his arms vertically above his head.

Touchdown, baby.

The visitors' side of the stadium erupts in applause and howling cheers.

Throat-tightening emotion washes over me, chiefly pride. I've worked so hard for this moment, and now it's here. Showcasing my talents, everything I was trained to do, in front of thousands of fans and millions of TV viewers . . . well, there's nothing else like it.

Even Alex slaps me on the back, laughing joyfully, his grudge about Jane apparently forgotten. And Jane herself is dancing like a maniac in the press box, stomping and cheering in victory right alongside us. Her ecstatic zeal makes me feel like I could fly.

• • •

By Monday, we're back to business as usual. Since we won the game, Coach Royce doesn't review tape with us. Instead, he just holds a quick team meeting to outline our agenda for the next week, and then congratulates us on all our hard work.

Afterward, I head to the weight room to train, more than ready to get back into my morning routine. I've just completed my last set of dead lifts and am about to move on to side planks when heavy footsteps approach behind me.

"What're you still doing here, Chase?" Coach Royce asks. "When I gave everyone the rest of the day off, that included you."

I lift the barbell back onto its rack with a loud grunt and turn to face him, wiping a towel across my damp forehead. "Can't slack off on strength training or I'll lose my gains. I'll go home as soon as I'm done."

He chuckles. "You haven't changed one bit. Always so deadly serious."

"Being serious is what wins games, Coach. Isn't that what you always used to tell me?" I take a swig of water.

"That it is, son." He gives me a proud smile. "And you've been doing amazing ever since. Especially in yesterday's game."

I duck my head. "Couldn't have done it if I hadn't had such a great coach."

He snorts at me, but the sound is familiar and fond. "Still humble too."

"No, I mean it. I don't know where I'd be without your help. Thanks for taking a chance on me." *Both taking me into the Hawks and teaching me the basics all those years ago.*

"Acquiring one of the country's best quarterbacks is hardly taking a chance. If the Rangers weren't already kicking themselves for losing you to the Hawks, they sure as shootin' are now."

I laugh and let the conversation trail into a moment of comfortable silence. I haven't really kept in touch with Coach Royce since college, and it's good to spend time together again. But there's something I want to know, even if it ruins the mood.

"So, uh . . . how's Jane?" I ask.

After our pregame sock-hunting mission that turned out to be such unexpected fun, I let myself hope that maybe the tension between us was starting to ease. But Jane spent the entire return flight next to her dad. She didn't so much as venture out of her seat, let alone come down the aisle to talk to me.

"Why don't you ask her yourself? She's right there." He points across the room to where Jane is peeking through the barely cracked door.

It's a good thing I'm not holding a weight anymore, because I might have dropped it on my foot.

Coach's mouth twists like he wants to laugh. "I'll be in my office. Gotta finish some paperwork before lunch." He winks and strolls away. "You kids have fun."

Jane slips through the door, and I can't tell if her slightly sheepish look is real or if I'm just projecting my own awkwardness. How long has she been watching us? Or was she watching *me*?

I walk over to her, feeling like I'm back in our high school gym and trying to work up the courage to ask her to dance. "Hey there."

"Hi." She sounds almost shy. "Congratulations on the game. That was quite a play."

"Thanks." I rub my neck.

She doesn't say anything else, but she also doesn't leave. The idea that she might be reluctant to go is probably too much to hope for. Is she waiting for me to say something? If so, what?

"Do something with me tomorrow," I blurt.

She blinks. "What?"

Well, that wasn't exactly how I would have wanted to say it, but the words leaped out of my mouth on their own, and now here we are.

I shrug. "I don't know. It's just, Tuesdays are our only day off, so . . ."

"No, I meant *what* as in, what did you have in

mind?"

I'll be damned . . . she actually sounds interested. Encouraged, I forge ahead. "How about that arcade we used to go to in high school?"

She shakes her head, frowning sadly. "It closed. That building's a bowling alley now."

"Even better. I love bowling. What do you say?"

"I say . . ." She taps her lips, considering. Then she flashes me a devilish smirk. "I say I'll destroy you."

I grin back at her. "Oh, really? If you're so confident, let's bet on it. We'll meet up at noon tomorrow, and if I win, you have to . . . hmm . . ." I rub my chin theatrically. "Do my laundry."

"Ew!" But she's giggling even as she wrinkles her nose. "And what about if I win?"

"I'll leave the prize up to you. Anything you want."

She hesitates, and for a moment I think she's going to tell me to fuck off. But then she surprises me yet again by nodding.

"All right. It's a bet." As she turns to open the

door, she adds, "Don't be late for your ass-whooping appointment."

"Oh, you are so on," I call after her. I wait until she's out of sight before I pump my fist.

Two big victories in two days . . . nothing can stop me.

CHAPTER Seven

Jane

The old arcade may be a bowling alley now, but nearly every other detail has remained precisely the same. There's the same geometric-patterned neon carpet beneath my wedges, the same suffocating smell of nacho cheese in the air, and the same quarterback waiting to meet me, filling my stomach with butterflies.

One quick scan of the room, and I spot Wes. He's already laid claim on a lane and has one foot up on a seat, trying to put on a bowling shoe that is clearly too small for his giant foot.

It's never exactly a game of "I Spy" trying to pick Wes out of a crowd since he's well over six feet tall. But today, there's no crowd to pick him out of. This place is a complete ghost town. I guess noon on a Tuesday isn't exactly a peak bowling hour.

Since Wes has his back to me, I gladly take the opportunity to take in the way his worn gray T-shirt hugs his perfectly carved back muscles. God, it's not even fair how ripped he is.

My mind wanders back to how he looked in the locker room, those shorts hanging off his waist, those deliciously defined abs on display as I tried not to stare. I'm surprised my jaw didn't hit the locker room floor.

But those daydreams will have to wait for now. I didn't come here to drool over Wes. I've got a bet to win.

By the time I saunter over to our lane, Wes has moved on to the second shoe. It looks like they're probably a size and a half too small. Two extra-large plastic cups from the snack bar sit on the table nearby, and since there's no one else in sight, I can safely assume they belong to him.

"Feeling extra thirsty?"

Wes looks up from his bowling shoes, his eyes flickering as they meet mine. "Unsweetened iced tea," he says, nodding toward the table. "Still your drink of choice or what?"

I reach for one of the oversized Styrofoam cups and take a big, long sip from the straw, a desperate attempt to cover the giddy smile threatening to spread across my face. How did he remember that?

"Hope you left room in your car for my big ol' hamper of dirty laundry, Royce," Wes says with a smirk, returning to loosening his laces. "Go get your shoes. I already paid for them."

The middle-aged guy behind the shoe counter has an eagle eye on me from the second I start heading his way. When I tell him my size, he leans over the counter like he's about to give me top-secret information. Not like there's anyone around to hear him.

"Hey, is your boyfriend Weston Chase, the new quarterback for the Hawks?"

I don't know what's more unnerving—the fact that this guy thinks Wes is my boyfriend, or how my palms tingle when he says it. I spent so many years introducing him with that title. My *boyfriend.* Now, I'm not even sure if today counts as a date. But I don't think the shoe-rental guy is the one to discuss this with, so I just play along.

"Yep. He sure is." I smile over my shoulder at Wes, who finally has his shoes on and is sizing up the racks of bowling balls, waiting for one to speak to him.

"Damn," the shoe guy says, shaking his head in disbelief as he sets my size sevens on the counter. "You're one lucky lady."

I tuck the shoes under my arm and hurry back to our lane, where Weston is holding a red bowling ball in one hand and a blue one in the other.

"Hawks colors," he says, obviously a little proud of himself. "Which color do you think is luckier?" His tone doesn't suggest a hint of sarcasm. Is he really going to take bowling as seriously as he takes football?

"Luck will get you nowhere, Chase," I say, playfully grabbing the red ball out of his hand. "But I know there's no way I'm washing your smelly laundry this week."

He cracks a smile that makes my knees buckle. "Bring it on, big shot."

Full disclosure . . . I can't even remember the last time I so much as stepped into a bowling alley, so I'm not sure why I talked such a big game yesterday. I'm relying solely on the handful of pointers I got on my two dates with the captain of the bowling team in college. Still, I put my bowling ball in the ball return and lace up my shoes like I do this every Tuesday. Fake it till you make it, right?

"Athletes first." I gesture to the lane as I slide into a seat, the bowling alley equivalent of watching Wes from the bleachers. I cup my iced tea in both hands, enjoying the view of Wes's butt in those dark-wash jeans as he lines up his shot and proceeds to roll the ball directly into the gutter.

I explode into a fit of giggles. "I'd better start thinking about what my prize is going to be," I call over the pop song blaring through the speakers.

Wes shoots me a glare, but he can't fool me. His mouth is twitching into a smile.

If there were a competition to hit the fewest number of pins, Weston Chase would be the MVP. Frame after frame, he rolls gutter balls like clockwork. Something in me isn't completely convinced that he's really this bad of a bowler. Maybe he's letting me win.

Either way, the game itself isn't half as fun as teasing him, joking that maybe he should have pursued a career in professional bowling instead of football. With every subsequent gutter ball, our laughter fills up every nook and cranny of this empty bowling alley. I can't remember the last time I laughed this hard.

It's not until I roll my last frame that it occurs to me that I haven't even glanced at the score the whole game. There's no point. Just about any double-digit score would have been enough to clinch my victory.

"It's a good thing you're not a kicker. I don't think we'd make a single field goal with that aim," I tease as Wes snags the seat next to me. The side of his thigh brushes against mine, but instead of pulling it back, he keeps it there, pressed snugly against me.

"I'll get you next time," he says, watching me. "And it'll be for two weeks of laundry."

"Oh yeah? Don't think I forgot about my prize," I coo, smiling devilishly. Me, forget about a bet? Not in a million years.

"What's it gonna be, Royce? Anything you want, it's yours."

Anything? My thoughts immediately scatter to a hundred places they shouldn't. I've been totally dropping the ball on my promise of staying away from Wes, but actually letting things go a step further . . . that's not something I could do. I've got to come up with something a little more PG than what

I really want.

Tilting my head, I look up at the ceiling thoughtfully and tap my chin for effect, but my train of thought is interrupted by the echoing grumble of Wes's stomach.

"How about we discuss it over some lunch?" I say. "Sounds like you might need it."

We return our rental shoes to the slack-jawed Hawks fan behind the counter as we discuss lunch options, eventually landing on the steakhouse across the street. Once again, the fact that it's early afternoon on a Tuesday is in our favor—we've got our pick of just about any table in the restaurant.

After we're seated, the waitress comes to ask what we'd like to drink, and Wes gestures for me to go ahead. We each order water with lemon, and then we're left alone.

"Today was fun." He grins at me.

I smile back, still unsure if he let me win on purpose.

The waitress returns with our drinks and pulls out a notepad. "What can I get you?"

Her gaze is on Wes, not an uncommon female response. I'm used to being completely ignored when in the presence of a pro athlete.

Wes suppresses a look of irritation and proceeds to order a T-bone steak dinner, a chicken sandwich, a large spinach salad, and a double order of cocktail shrimp. The waitress can hardly keep up, frantically scribbling down the order.

"Is . . . is that for both of you?" she asks, wide-eyed. I'm guessing she doesn't serve a lot of football players here.

"Nope." Wes grins proudly. "Jane, go ahead."

"Just the chicken sandwich for me," I say politely.

The waitress sighs in relief for the sake of her cramping hand, then rushes off to the kitchen to put in the order for more food than she probably eats in a week. I can't blame her for being so surprised. With all the time I spend with the team, nothing surprises me anymore.

When our food arrives, we waste no time in digging in. I guess all that bowling helped us both work up an appetite. Wes puts away the whole steak, half the salad, and an order of shrimp before I've made it through my chicken sandwich. I almost feel like I should applaud.

"So, I've got to ask." He wipes a napkin across his mouth. "How has the dating scene been for you? After, you know." He fusses with his napkin, dodging eye contact. "I know that my love-life drama has been all over the tabloids lately. But what about you? Anyone serious?"

"Only one serious relationship. We were dating at the very end of college, and then for the first year or so after, but he wanted to move in together. And I, well . . ." I shrug, waving a steak fry through the air. "He just wasn't the one, I guess. But pretty much nothing since then. A few blind-date setups, but that's about it."

Wes nods, his mouth pressed into a straight line. "Just can't find anyone worth your time?"

"Whatever little time I have," I say, then pop a fry into my mouth. "And I'm hardly even in town with all the away games during the season. I barely have time to take care of myself. Is it cliché to say I'm married to my job?"

Wes smirks and steals a fry off my plate. "A little. But I'll let it slide." He drops the smile and gets a serious look in his eyes. "You really should make some time for yourself, though. You deserve it."

"Actually, that gives me a great idea." I steal a shrimp off his plate, making us even for the stolen fry.

Wes only smiles.

"Consider it the first part of my prize. Now, you better hurry up and finish eating so we can get to the second part."

Wes happily accepts my challenge, finishing the rest of his food in ten minutes flat, hardly leaving time to breathe between bites. Honestly, he might have a career in competitive eating if he ever retires from football. He grabs the check, which I don't argue with considering the cost of his meal compared to mine, and we're out the door.

Next stop—my apartment.

It's a quick drive across town with Wes trailing behind me in his rental car, but I appreciate the few minutes alone to get my mind right. Spending time one-on-one with Wes in public felt shockingly natural, but being alone with him at my place is a totally different challenge. I know I have to be careful around him, and bringing him back to my empty apartment isn't exactly the definition of being careful.

Still, a bet is a bet, and I'm not letting him off

the hook without keeping up his end of the deal.

"Home sweet home," I say as I swing open the front door of my apartment.

Much like everything else in my life, my place is all about the Hawks. Not in a man-cave way, of course, but the red and navy accents in every otherwise all-white room are a quiet nod at the best team on the planet. I gesture for Wes to grab a seat on the leather couch, then run upstairs and return with a bottle of bright red nail polish.

"Am I giving you a manicure?" Wes asks, one eyebrow cocked.

"Close. Pedicure," I say with a satisfied grin. "After all, you said I should make more time for myself. So you're going to help me do just that." I slip out of my wedges and take a seat next to Wes, wiggling my toes and holding out the bottle of polish. "Ready when you are."

It takes him a minute to figure out how to even get the bottle of polish open. The little red bottle looks so funny and small in his big, fumbling hands. He looks up at me several times, seeking help, but I'm having way too good of a time watching him try.

Once he finally gets the bottle open, he slips

down to the floor and grasps my left foot. A shiver runs through me as he cradles it in his hand, the pads of his fingers pressed gently into the arch.

Wow. It's been way too long since a man has touched me. Something I clearly underestimated the need for until this precise moment.

He gets to work painting in slow, shaky strokes. You'd think he was painting the Sistine Chapel with that kind of laser focus.

Despite his best efforts, he's getting nail polish on the skin next to my toenails, but I'm too wrapped up in his touch to care. His calloused fingers ease up to my ankle as he finishes my pinkie toe, then he raises my foot and blows a steady stream of air across my painted nails.

Fuck. Suddenly, my nail polish isn't the only thing that's wet.

"That's how you dry them, right?" He glances up at me with a sultry look.

I know he isn't looking for an answer. The man knows exactly what he's doing to me. Having him paint my nails was supposed to be silly, not sexy, yet here I am trying to keep from moaning in pleasure.

Seeing him on his knees like this, I'm not surprised when my memory flickers back to a few other times we were in this position. I used to sit on the edge of the futon in his mom's basement while he knelt in front of me, exploring the space between my thighs. I remember the first time, when he told me he'd never done this before and I said neither had I, but he devoured every inch of me like I was the sweetest thing he'd ever tasted.

I wonder if he remembers that as well as I do. A part of me hopes he's thinking about it right now too. *God, what is wrong with me?*

Once he's done, he lowers my foot gently, like he's setting down a newborn kitten, then moves on to the other foot. The thumb of his left hand kneads at the arch of my foot as his right hand paints. A foot rub wasn't part of my prize, but I won't turn it down. This time, when he blows cool air across my toenails, I'm ready for it, but it's still sexy as hell watching him do this.

"All done," he says softly. "How'd I do?"

"F-fine," I stutter, not even looking at my toes to check his work. "Thanks."

"You won it fair and square." He pushes himself off the floor and rejoins me on the couch, his leg once again pressing firmly into mine. "But I'll get you next time. I don't think you'll be doing my laundry, though. I can think of something way better."

"Oh yeah? Like what?" Why is my voice so husky?

Wes leans in toward me and my breathing hitches. Both of us freeze there, our faces inches apart. Are we really doing this? Wes hesitates, bites down hard on his lower lip, and turns my head with his fingertips before planting a gentle kiss on my cheek.

"It's probably best that I get out of here," he mutters into my ear.

My shoulders sag. The last thing I want is for him to leave, but I scrunch my eyes closed and give him a sad nod.

"Yeah. You should go." I sigh, opening my eyes and meeting his gaze.

The look in his eyes is disappointed, if not a little sad, but he's right. Cutting things off here is the smart thing to do.

But, God, do I hate being smart sometimes.

Chapter Eight

Weston

I don't see Jane at all on Wednesday. Not at the morning meeting, not during training workouts, not at lunch, not at my practice drills. Which gives me plenty of time to work myself up into a neurotic lather, wondering what her disappearance means.

I thought yesterday's date went pretty well—no, not a date, our totally platonic hangout, I correct myself for the thousandth time. But now I have no idea what's going on in her head.

Is she avoiding me? Did I somehow fuck everything up again? Or maybe she's not even thinking about me at all. I guess that possibility is better than her being mad at me, but it doesn't sting much less.

Holy shit, man, get a grip.

This is a meaningless coincidence. She's probably just busy with paperwork or something. Or maybe she's sick. But if she's sick, maybe I should go check on . . .

Dammit, no! Just chill out and do your job.

I continue stewing all evening and well into Thursday afternoon. I try to channel my nerves and distract myself by going all-out in practice. When Coach Royce blows his whistle to signal the end of our final drill, I take off my helmet and wipe my sweaty face . . . only to see Jane walking toward me across the field, carrying a flat plastic box.

My stomach gives a little jump. I stop and wait for her to catch up to me. Just seeing her again is a bigger relief than I thought. Even better, she doesn't look mad—although I don't know what that hard-set determined expression means.

She stops at arm's length. Without preamble, she says, "I baked cookies last night." The words come a little too fast to match her nonchalant tone. "I was bored, I guess. But you'd better take these, otherwise I'll eat them all and make myself sick, and . . . Ugh, here." She thrusts the box at me like it's a weapon. Or a shield.

"Oh. Um, thank you." I take it and am surprised at how heavy it is.

The intense scents of chocolate and peanuts greet me as I open the lid. The box is packed full of a dozen enormous fudge cookies, made with so much cocoa they're almost black, studded with dark chocolate chips and streaked with golden-brown peanut butter. They look—and smell—freaking amazing.

For a moment, I'm speechless that Jane still remembers my favorite kind of cookie. I've always had a major sweet tooth, especially for chocolate, but this clinches my suspicions. She baked these specifically for me.

And although she's fidgeting, she's not walking away. She's still standing here, waiting for more of my reaction.

Well, don't mind if I do.

I whip out a cookie on the spot and take a big bite, savoring the dense, rich sweetness, then hold it out to her. "Have some?"

She shakes her head. "Thanks, but I'm not hungry."

"Come on, Janie, just one little taste. You put

all that work into baking them, you deserve at least part of the reward. And they're really delicious . . ." I wiggle the cookie to tempt her.

Her gaze flicks between me and her gift for a moment. Then she sighs. "Oh, all right, if you're offering. They do smell really good."

I expect her to take the rest of the cookie from my hand, but she leans forward and bites it while I'm still holding it. She lets out a very quiet, but definitely happy sigh as she chews. Chocolatey crumbs decorate her lips and even the tip of her nose. It's incredibly cute.

It's hard to resist the urge to kiss her face clean, and impossible to resist asking, "Can I get your phone number?"

She blinks, and I hurriedly make it into a joke by adding, "You know, in case you need any more help painting your nails."

She snorts, holding back a smile. "Awesome. My own personal mani-pedi guy."

"That's me." I look around for something to write it down with.

Dammit. I always leave my phone in my locker during practice, and I don't see a single pencil or piece of paper on the field, because why the hell would there be? Not even a frigging pen to write it on my hand.

"Um . . ." She chews her lip. "How about I text you? I should probably have yours too, anyway, since we work together."

She pulls her phone from her pocket, pokes at it, and holds it out to me. I can't type in my number fast enough.

When I get back to my locker, her text is waiting for me. It's just a quick *hi Wes, it's Jane*, but even a tiny win is still a win, and it gives me hope that many more will come.

I grin as I save her number to my contacts.

• • •

Well, that hope didn't last long. A week and a half later, and Jane still hasn't called or texted me, not even about Hawks business.

I've thought about contacting her plenty of times, but I always hit the same dead end. What would I say? I have no excuse to talk to her, no plausible topic of conversation. And I refuse to be that guy who sends girls half-assed texts like *hey* or *wyd?* or God forbid, *u up?* with a winky-face emoji. Jesus save us all.

So I always ended up waffling for half an hour, then shoving my phone back in my pocket. And now I'm staring at a hotel room ceiling, trying to *go the fuck to sleep already* so I won't ruin our chances against the Cobras tomorrow. But I'm failing miserably because I'm way too aware that Jane's room is right next to mine.

Right.

Fucking.

Next.

To.

Mine.

Dear God, this is torture.

I shake my head at my own ridiculousness. No, it's idiotic is what it is. I clearly just need to get laid.

I haven't had sex since Trista, so it's natural that I can't stop thinking about it, and the solution is obvious. But the thought of going out to score with some random jersey chaser is totally unappealing.

The only woman I want right now is the one I

can't have. The woman I've been kicking myself about losing for the last ten years. The woman on the other side of a thin hotel wall, not even two yards away. There's even an adjoining door, just to really bust my balls.

I look at the clock and groan. It's almost midnight. I need to do something, anything to fix this, but what? Drink the minibar and then try to play with a hangover tomorrow? Borrow the team's rental car and embark on a wild goose chase for over-the-counter sleeping pills that never help anyway?

Hell, I can't even distract myself by talking strategy with Colin, because he's always early to get to bed, just like half the team—and good for them. The other half are busy sneaking girls past security and into their rooms for hookups.

I'm all alone with my stupid thoughts, feeling lonely, and if I'm honest, horny. I think I'm going to punch something. Maybe the wall. Yeah, punch right through the wall into Jane's room and—

Letting out a frustrated growl, I roll out of bed and onto my feet, then pull my clothes back on. *Fuck it.*

Besides, I'm not doing myself any favors by

getting all worked up so late at night. If I can't sleep anyway, I might as well do what I really want to do and go talk to Jane. Maybe then I'll be able to calm down.

This probably isn't a good idea. I already know that. But before I can come to my senses, I step out into the hallway and knock on Jane's door.

And when it opens to Jane standing there in her cute Hawks-patterned pajamas, her golden hair in a messy ponytail, toothbrush in her mouth . . . I stop caring.

CHAPTER *Nine*

Jane

It's ten thirty and I'm about ready to call it a night when there's a knock on my door.

Did I order room service and forget? I kind of hope so. I wouldn't say no to a late-night snack, even if I am halfway through brushing my teeth. I spit toothpaste foam into the sink, turn off the faucet, and wipe my mouth with the back of my hand.

"Who is it?"

"It's me," a male voice says.

My heart leaps in my chest. Wes. He's cutting it close to curfew, and I'm not exactly looking like a beauty queen in my pajama shorts and oversized Hawks shirt, but the thought of seeing him sends a tingle of excitement up my spine.

When I open the door, I'm reassured to see that Wes is rocking his PJs too—baggy black sweatpants hang off his lean hips, and his round biceps bulge out of the fitted sleeves of a Hawks tee, a match to the one I've got on. It's part of the standard swag bag all new players and Hawks employees get. His is still new compared to mine, which is so faded you can hardly make out the team logo anymore.

"Nice shirt," I say.

"You too. Can I come in?"

I frown, trying to read the expression on his face. "What's going on? Pregame jitters?"

Wes shoves his hands into his sweatpants pockets and looks down at his socks. "Something like that."

My gaze darts up and down the hallway. No coaches or other players are in sight, so I guess there's no harm in letting him in for a bit. I open the door the rest of the way, motioning him in as I head to the bathroom to finish brushing my teeth.

I study my reflection as I swish mouthwash between my cheeks. Messy bun, no makeup, the last freckles of summer sprinkled over my nose and cheeks. It's a far cry from the perfectly tousled waves and full face of makeup I had on for our bowling date. Still, despite my escalated heart rate, the girl in the mirror looks calm and collected, not at all like there's a professional football player lounging on her bed. Let's hope Wes is fooled too.

When I emerge from the bathroom, I find Wes lying on his stomach, chin in hand, flipping through the channels. He looks like a gossipy middle school girl at a sleepover. I imagine him in fuzzy pink bunny slippers, and the thought makes me giggle.

"Something funny about home renovation?" he asks, referring to the do-it-yourself decorating show he's landed on.

"There's something funny about you picking out this show out of a hundred channels." I sit on the bed next to him, the fluffy white comforter giving way with a soft puff of air.

I never would have guessed just a few short weeks ago that I would find myself in the same hotel room, let alone the same bed, as Weston Chase. And yet here we are, just inches apart, both of us clearly trying to act like this is totally normal.

"Shouldn't you be watching ESPN or something? Studying up like a good football player?" I tease.

Wes shakes his head, pushing himself up so he's seated cross legged, his knees pushed up against mine. "It's all Rangers talk. And a lot of it is just bullshit rumors about me and why I left. I don't want to hear it."

I nod, thinking about what Dad told me the day before Wes signed, that his ex-fiancée cheated on him with another Ranger. The tabloids seem to be running with that story, although every one of them wants to take it in a different direction. One magazine says there was a pregnancy scandal, another says they were already married and are in the throes of a pricey divorce. I've avoided the topic like the plague, but now that he's opened the door, I guess I might as well ask the source himself.

"If you want to talk, I'm here," I say. "After all, you asked me about my past relationships, so it's only fair." When he doesn't say anything, I quickly add, "Unless you don't want to talk about it, which I would totally understand."

"Nah, it's cool. It's not a secret or anything." Wes shrugs, looking down at his socks again. "I wish some of these dumb gossip columns would be that straightforward with me and just ask for the truth. They've got the basic story down, though. My ex-fiancée was sleeping with another player.

A linebacker. I walked in on them on the couch of our apartment. I'd gotten out of a press conference earlier than I told her I would, and thought I'd surprise her . . ." He trails off, swallowing a lump in his throat. It's clearly still an open wound.

Shit. Now I feel bad that I've opened this can of worms.

"In your own apartment? God, I'm so sorry, Wes. I can't even imagine."

I instinctively reach out and lay my hand on top of his. It's a risky move, and I know I should pull away, but Wes meets my touch with a sad, soft smile. He rotates his hand so our palms face each other, his thumb lazily tracing the lines of my palm.

"Let's talk about something else. Let's talk about you. You're way more interesting than me."

I throw my head back with a laugh, which brings back that familiar twinge in my back, making me grimace. Too much time spent hunched over my desk this week.

"You okay?" Wes asks, his hand freezing in mine.

"No, it's not you. It's my back. It's been killing me."

Wes furrows his brow, releasing my hand to reach for the phone in his sweatpants pocket. "Do you want me to text the team masseuse? I'm sure she can fit you in."

A giggle escapes from the back of my throat. "Do you think I can pass as a linebacker? Because I think that's a players-only perk."

"Oh, come on." He playfully nudges my knee with his, and I try to act unaffected by his touch. "I'm sure they'd make an exception for the head coach's daughter."

"No way," I say seriously, my joking tone gone. "I never, ever use that to my advantage. Back pain or no back pain." I grimace again as I press my thumb into the center of the knot in my neck. A massage really would help, but I'm far too stubborn to work my connections to get ahead.

"Fine." Wes smirks, his eyes narrowing. He's spotted a challenge. "Then let me do it."

I know I should protest. If Wes gets his hands on me, I know I'll be done for, totally unable to hold back from him any longer, but the twinge in my back is making a pretty good argument. If it hurts this much for the game tomorrow, I'll be completely useless. Obviously, the best thing I can do from a work standpoint is let Weston Chase rub my back. Right?

"Fine." I surrender, situating myself so my back is facing him. "But just for a few minutes. And then I've gotta go to bed."

Without another word, Wes begins working his hands up and down my back through my oversized shirt. He finds every knot without any guidance, kneading each one with dexterous thumbs.

Holy shit, he's good. I thought the pedicure was nice, but this is a whole new level of heavenly. His thumbs trace the edges of my shoulder blades, and even through the worn fabric of my shirt, it's enough to make my toes curl.

"Let's get rid of this." Wes tugs gently at my shirt. "It'll make things easier."

I turn my head and shoot him a knowing *don't go there* look.

"It's in the way!" he says defensively. Like I'm supposed to believe he has no other intentions. "And I won't look, I promise." He smirks, then adds, "Anyway, I've seen it all before," which earns him a slap on the shoulder.

"All right, all right," he says. "Fine. Over the

shirt, it is."

He turns me back around, returning to his task. All those years of gripping the laces of a football have done him a few favors. Those fingers know exactly how to hold me.

I feel his breath against the back of my neck as he leans into an especially tight muscle. A low hum of satisfaction escapes my lips as his steady, sure hands work down my back and find their grip on my hips.

Shit. I can't help but give in to those hands. He's got a hold on me in more ways than one. I feel my shoulders relax into him as he pulls me closer, tilting me back, reclining me into his lap so my chin is lifted toward his.

Wes watches me, probably waiting for me to stop this. I don't.

Then he presses his mouth against mine.

Holy shit. This isn't the man I kissed ten years ago.

This man is more certain, tilting my chin to whatever angle suits him best as his lips mold themselves to mine. He still remembers the way I like to be kissed, gently at first, then more deeply.

Against my better judgment, I let my hand float up to his cheek, brushing my fingertips across his stubble as his tongue flirts with mine.

Tugging oh-so-gently at my lower lip with his teeth, he pulls away just far enough to get a good look at me, his calloused fingers tracing the outline of my jaw. I know I'm a mess of bed head and under-eye circles, but he gazes down at me like I'm a masterpiece, and I can't help but feel beautiful. I wish this moment would never end, that we could stay frozen here and forget about reality, about our messy past.

"What happened to us?" he whispers, twirling a strand of my hair that has escaped from my messy bun before tucking it behind my ear. "We really had something. Why did we lose it?"

My heart sinks to the bottom of my stomach. *Welcome back to reality, Jane*. It's almost curfew the night before a big game. Are we really going to have this conversation *now*?

I toy with the idea of telling him I don't know what happened, or pretending that it was too long ago for me to remember the details. Maybe I could wave off his question and coax him into kissing me again. It would be better that way. Safer. But it wouldn't be fair. And if he's brave enough to be honest with me about his ex-fiancée, the least I can do is muster up the courage to tell him the truth.

"Are you sure you want to know?" I ask, giving him one last out. I don't want him to be distracted on the field tomorrow.

"I *need* to know."

Shit. I shimmy loose from Wes's arms, unfolding myself from him as I turn so we're sitting knee to knee.

"It's more complicated than you think, Wes," I say softly, picking at a loose thread on my T-shirt to avoid making eye contact. "And I don't want to throw you off before the game. Let's just go to bed, talk about it tomorrow."

Wes cups my chin, tilting it up until my eyes meet his. His gaze is paralyzing. How could I say no to him?

"Jane. Whatever it is, you can tell me. I need to know."

Easy for him to say. He's not the one with shaky hands and a quivering lower lip. He's not the one who has to say it out loud.

My breathing stutters. There's no easy way to say this, no smooth path through the truth. Might as well just blurt it out, get it over with.

"Wes, I . . . I was pregnant."

The silence that follows is deafening, those three words hovering in the space between us. There. I said it. The truth I've been hanging on to for the last decade. Now the secret isn't just mine to hold anymore. It's both terrifying and exhilarating.

"You . . . you were pregnant?"

Tears threaten to roll down my cheeks, so I squeeze my eyes tight, barricading them in for a few moments longer as I give Wes a tiny nod.

"With my baby?"

Of course, you dipshit. I nod again.

"Why didn't you tell me, Jane?" His tone is stern, almost angry.

But if it's an explanation he wants, it's an explanation he'll get. The words come tumbling out like marbles, and once I start, I can't stop.

"I tried to tell you. I called you as soon as I found out, but you had some big football party you were going to. You kept ignoring my calls, sending me these stupid short texts that you couldn't talk.

Don't you remember?"

I give him a chance to recall, to carry on the story from his point of view, but he just gives me a halfhearted shrug, his gaze downcast. He really doesn't remember this at all. Part of me is envious, wishing I could forget too.

"When you finally picked up, I was practically begging you to drive home that weekend, telling you we needed to talk," I say. "You didn't have a game, just football parties and dumb stuff like that. I told you I needed you here, needed you home. And I'll never forget, you said, 'I've got to focus on football. Maybe in a couple of weeks.' And you hung up. That's when I knew. I saw your future, and I saw that I didn't fit into it, that you wouldn't sacrifice your plans for me, for our baby. Football would always come first. That's why I broke things off."

And he didn't even fight for me.

I take a long, slow breath, filling my completely emptied lungs. I'm waiting for him to say something, anything, even just a nod, but for what feels like forever, Wes remains frozen, the only movement in the room coming from the slight vibration of his clenched jaw.

Finally, he gives me a response. It's the question I knew he'd ask.

"What happened to my baby, Jane?" His voice is slow and wavering, muffled by his tensed jaw.

"*Our* baby," I say, correcting him. The tears come steadily now, streaming down my cheeks, and I don't try to stop them. "Our baby hardly made it a couple of weeks. I wasn't even far enough along to tell my parents, to tell anybody. And then I woke up one morning and there was all this blood, and I drove myself to the clinic . . ."

I wipe the tears off my cheeks with the back of my hand, pushing down the memories of the harsh fluorescent lights, the scratchy paper gown, the apologetic look on the doctor's face when he returned with the news. I can't give Wes every detail. I'll fall apart if I do.

"I was so alone, Wes," I manage to say through sniffles. "I was alone and scared and angry. I was angry with you, angry with my body. I knew I couldn't tell you, couldn't tell anyone. I mean, I was barely eighteen. And I'd just lost the love of my life."

Silence again. But I have nothing more to say. I take a minute to steady my breath before looking over at him. His gaze is glued to the floor, his hands clenched into two white-knuckled fists, a grip so tight he could crush stone in his palms.

"Wes?" I say his name meekly, hoping he'll at least look at me, but there's nothing. Only the flare of his nostrils, the harsh sound of his quickening breath.

Is he angry? If anyone has the right to be angry here, it's me, not him. I'm the one who had to go through hell and back while he was off drinking at some stupid college football party.

"Wes, please say something." I'm desperate now.

I gave him the explanation he wanted, even though it meant staring down the memories I've tried to suppress for so long. And now what? Nothing. Not a word.

Can't he at least look at me? Anything? Just moments ago, he was holding me in his arms like I was his prized possession. Now, it's like there's a wall between us, and I would do anything to knock it down.

Without so much as a glance at me, he swings his legs over the side of the bed and heads for the door.

“Wes, please.” I squeak out the words in one last pathetic attempt, but it’s not enough to keep him here. The only sound he makes is the click of the door closing as he leaves.

My shoulders heave as I release the sob I’ve been holding back, and I let myself collapse into the padded space of the comforter that still holds his shape.

I’m alone. Again. And it almost hurts worse this time, because this time, he knows what he’s leaving.

CHAPTER Ten

Weston

Disgusted with myself, I wrench my locker open and rip off my jersey. The Cobras annihilated us, twenty-nine to six. Maybe they would have won no matter what, but they sure wouldn't have stomped us so hard if I'd been able to focus worth a damn.

I couldn't make sense of anything that was going on. The action that I normally flow through so easily was choppy chaos. I was sloppy. Useless. I haven't played that badly since high school.

What the fuck happened?

I know exactly what happened. I couldn't stop thinking about what Jane said last night. It kept banging around and around my head until all I could see was her angry tears, all I could hear was her teenage voice on my phone, cracking as she pleaded . . . as she told me she needed me.

This is the first time the Hawks have taken a loss since I joined the team, so I don't know how things normally go with them. But the locker room is dead silent, only the clank of lockers and the hiss of showers. Everyone is avoiding each other . . . or maybe just me. Not even Colin has given me so much as a slap on the shoulder.

Well, good. Let them all stay away. Fuck this city and everyone in it, especially me. I want to be alone. I want to suffer in the knowledge that I left Jane out in the cold, all those years ago.

My hand clenches on the locker door. That's not fair. I had no idea she was pregnant. Never even suspected it. If I'd known, I would have done things totally differently. Right?

Of course I would have.

But a quiet, nasty voice at the back of my mind whispers, *Are you sure?*

Obviously, I was an immature dipshit back then. I'm mature enough now to see and admit just how immature I used to be. But even as a dumb teenager, I still would have done the right thing and stepped up to the plate. Even though the idea of quitting football makes me feel like throwing myself off a cliff, I would have dropped out of school to go home and help take care of Jane and the baby. Acted like a real man, a real father. Not like mine. Nothing like the man who knocked up my mom and then ran off to God knows where, abandoned his wife and child . . .

Or maybe there's a piece of him inside you after all.

I slam my locker shut and stalk off to the showers. I need to stop thinking. My body protests as I scrub off the sweat and dirt and failure. I'm a mess of sore muscles and bruises after taking tackles from what felt like every single Cobra on the field, but I'm too pissed off to really feel the pain.

"Well, that sure was a shit show, wasn't it?" Colin says from the stall next to me.

I can't muster more than an irritable grunt. The guy on my other side edges away slightly. I probably look about two seconds away from murder.

I know I shouldn't be, but I'm so fucking mad at Jane right now, I can feel it deep in my bones. She just cut our relationship off at the knees back then, without telling me what was really going on.

How could she hide something so huge from me? How can she blame me for not helping her when I didn't even know she needed help?

"I'm a trustworthy guy, right?" I ask abruptly.

"What?" Colin sounds baffled. "Where's this coming from?"

Crap. How do I explain without getting into details? I choose my next words carefully.

"Somebody I knew in college said sh—said they once had a problem. A really big one. But I had no idea they were dealing with it until they got upset at me for doing nothing."

"Well, did they tell you about it?"

"I just said I had no idea what was going on with them."

"That doesn't mean they didn't tell you."

"What?" I'm worn out and starting to regret speaking up at all.

"You can get really wrapped up in things. Which is great for the team, but sometimes you go a little nuts. Especially if we're talking about when we were in college, seems like you were always preoccupied back then. It was like you couldn't see anything but football."

"And Jane?"

Colin makes an uncertain *eh* noise. "To be honest, dude, I didn't even know you had a girlfriend until our first semester was almost over."

My hands pause in lathering my hair. I talked that little about Jane? I spent that little time with her?

No way. She was my first love. The center of my world.

But did I act like it?

Sure, I forgot to text her sometimes, and I had to flake out on a few phone dates. And even when we did hang out, I talked mostly in monosyllables and grunts . . .

Okay, so I acted like kind of a dumbass back then. But it's not that I didn't care about her. I just had so much on my plate—my head too full of homework and football plays, my body too tired from practice drills and late nights studying.

Still, I can't deny that I neglected her. From her point of view, it must have felt like we were drifting apart. Hell, maybe she even thought I was getting bored with her. Gearing up to move on.

That's ridiculous. Jane could never bore me.

But did *she* know that? Plenty of long-distance relationships fall apart in that exact way. Especially when people are at college, surrounded by new responsibilities and distractions.

That whisper in my mind is starting to sound less cruel and more wise, but I still make one last attempt to defend myself.

Of course she knew I loved her. I told her she was my best girl all the time.

The sweetest words are still just words, though. When it came time to put my money where my mouth was, when she was lost, begging for help, scared out of her mind, I blew her off. And for what? A fucking party. At the time, that initiation ceremony seemed like the most crucial event in history, my best opportunity to network and become a real part of the team . . . but fundamentally, it was still just a party.

I didn't listen. As the truth dawns on me, my insides turn to ice. Of course, I hadn't realized she was trying to tell me something important, because all I'd been thinking about was getting to that stupid party on time.

She wasn't the one who didn't give *me* a

chance. It was the other way around.

God, no wonder she felt like I didn't give a shit about her. No wonder she decided to cut her losses. No wonder she's been so pissed at me ever since I joined the Hawks.

"You still with us, bro?" Colin asks.

I nod, even though he's on the other side of the wall and can't see me. "It's nothing. I'm fine."

It's everything, and I'm terrible. And Jane must feel a hundred times worse right now.

"If you say so. Long as you don't have a concussion." Colin sounds skeptical, but he's a *live and let live* kind of guy, not the type to pry. "I'm gonna go back to the hotel and get dinner before we roll. See you there?"

"Nah, I'm not hungry." I just want an excuse to shut myself in our room and not have to talk to anyone.

Colin whistles some pop song off-key as he walks back to his locker.

I have to fix this. But my mistakes have festered in her heart for so many years, I really hope I can figure out a way. I can't stand it when Jane is upset. I need to win her approval and forgiveness in a way I've never felt before. I've missed her so much, and it's all hitting me right now.

I shut off the shower, still feeling dirty. A hard, bitter lump forms in my throat, and I feel like puking. I almost wish I would, just to get rid of this feeling. I know that won't help, though . . . but I know what will.

As I get dressed, I text Jane.

`Can we talk?`

• • •

She hasn't answered.

Of course not, stupid, did you really expect her to? I stuff my phone back in my pocket.

I'm losing my mind. It's been a long twenty-four hours, but I don't feel any better now that we're back home.

Colin hits PAUSE on the remote. "Dude, I don't know what's going on with you, and you don't have to tell me if you don't want, but can you at least sit still? You're missing the best part."

"Shut it," I reply.

I set my phone facedown on the coffee table to attempt to focus on the movie he's showing me—according to him, the best horror action comedy ever made. But I have no idea what's going on, because I've been checking my phone every five fucking minutes like some kind of lovesick teenager instead of watching.

My attention soon starts wandering. I sneak another glance at my phone. Maybe just one more . . .

It dings, and I almost launch my bowl of popcorn across the room.

"Jesus!" Colin yells, startled. Spilled beer spreads over his shirt. "What the hell, man?"

"Sorry." I toss a roll of paper towels at him and fumble for my phone to read the message I've been waiting for.

`You free now?`

Hell yes, I am. I could be getting eaten by a grizzly bear right this second, and I'd find a way to see Jane.

`Yeah, where are you?`

`Just got home. Had to deal with some paperwork.`

Seriously, right after an away game? She works too hard. As I debate whether I should invite her here, another message appears.

`Come over?`

I type *on my way* and stand up. “I gotta go.”

“What, right now? Why?” Colin looks confused and sounds annoyed, a rarity for the most laid-back guy I’ve ever met. “The movie’s almost over.”

“I have to go meet Jane. It’s important,” I say, already halfway to the door.

His eyebrows fly up and he nods sagely. “Oh.”

I’m not sure what he’s imagining, and I don’t really care. I snag a bottle of wine from our fridge on my way out. I can pay Colin back later.

A talk like this needs a peace offering.

• • •

As soon as Jane opens her apartment door, I blurt,

"I was a massive dickhead."

She blinks owlishly at me. Still in her travel-rumpled work clothes, she apparently wasn't kidding about just now getting home.

"Uh . . . that's a good start. But maybe come in before you start yelling cuss words, so the neighbors don't call the cops?" She steps back to allow me inside, then shuts the door behind me and locks it.

I hold up the bottle. "I brought wine."

She accepts it without smiling. After pouring two glasses, she puts the bottle in the fridge.

I head to the living room. The last time I was here, I was so preoccupied with her, that I barely took the time to notice, but the walls are plastered with Hawks jerseys, helmets, autographed posters, newspaper clippings, pictures of famous players shaking hands with her dad, and every other kind of memorabilia imaginable.

Jane turns and thrusts a glass at me. "Here," she says, her tone neutral.

I take it and follow her to the couch. Things are still tense, and Jane sits as far away from me as possible. My gaze wanders to the end table, where there's a framed family photo. It takes a minute to recognize Ken, her dad, with a full head of hair, and I haven't seen Nancy since high school. But Jane's mom looks just like the Midwestern housewife I remember—calm brown eyes, a round, kindly face, the honey-colored hair that Jane inherited. A tiny Jane, maybe six years old and wearing a flowered romper, sprawls giggling over their laps.

I suddenly wonder if our baby would have looked like that.

"So, what were you wanting to say?" Jane asks, thankfully pulling me away from that uncomfortable, but strangely compelling thought.

I clear my throat. "I'm sorry. I handled this whole thing really badly. I should've listened and been supportive, but instead I just stormed out. I wasn't thinking." I'm not sure if I mean I wasn't thinking last night or ten years ago. Probably both.

Jane swallows hard, not meeting my eyes. "I get it. You were just . . . shocked, so you . . . overreacted."

More like devastated and blamed the real victim in this whole situation.

"Yeah, I was, but that's no excuse for just storming out. You were trying to tell me something really personal and painful and tough, and I made it all about me." I huff out an exhale. "Seems like I have a way of doing that. But now that I've had some time to think, I understand why you did what you did."

She finally looks at me. "You do?" Her tone is ever so slightly hopeful, but her eyes are still wary. Vulnerable.

"I mean, I don't know exactly how you felt, but it must have been horrible. You were trying to get through school when suddenly this huge, terrifying thing happened, and I made you feel like you couldn't count on me . . . like you had to face it alone." Almost without thinking, I reach out to rest my hand on hers. "I can't imagine going through something like that."

For a minute, she doesn't move. Whether she wants the touch or just tolerates it, I don't know. But she doesn't push me away, and that's a hell of a lot better than before.

Then she swallows hard. "Wes . . ." Her voice is raspy, choked. Her eyes glisten, and she blinks rapidly. "Thank you."

"I'm only saying what I should have said last night—I'm so sorry. I hate that I wasn't there for you."

Jane's face crumples. She lets me pull her into my arms and burrows her face into my chest. God, it's been so long since I've held her, yet somehow it still feels so fucking right.

The feel of her slender body encircled in my arms brings back a flood of memories I'm not prepared for. Memories of stolen moments and hot kisses, and more first times than I can count on two hands. Of starry nights and football games, and I-love-yous exchanged under the bleachers. Memories of my fingers fumbling with the clasp of her bra, her eager noises when I finally dared to slip my hand into her panties for the first time. The flush of her cheeks and the wetness between her legs, and the smug satisfaction that I'd done that to her made pride blossom in my chest, even more than when I threw a touchdown pass to win the game.

I possessively worked her toward orgasm, issuing my own deep groan of pleased satisfaction when I made her come for the first time.

I was an overexcited sixteen-year-old with a new driver's license and the hottest girlfriend in school. But Jane never made me feel like anything less than a man. I recalled the determined look in her eyes when she popped the button on my jeans that first time. My helpless plea when she ran the palm of her hand over the length of my hard shaft, looking down at me in wonder.

During the awkward fumbling as she tested the weight of my cock in her hand, I bit back a groan, more than happy to let her explore.

"Show me how to do it," she whispered.

I licked my lips and kissed her once more, taking her right hand in mine and curling it around my shaft.

That night I learned the bliss of someone else's hand jacking me. But not just anyone, the girl I loved.

"We need to stop, or I'm about to make a big fucking mess," I groaned.

Jane didn't stop, though, didn't let up, and then I came all over her hand in a hot, sticky mess. She balled up her tank top and handed it to me. I wiped myself clean, and she went home that night wearing my sweatshirt with nothing else underneath it.

God, it feels like just yesterday in some ways. I tug her closer, those familiar possessive feelings stirring inside me as her cheek nestles against the side of my neck.

Even though she's stopped crying, I know all of this is my fault, and I wish I had a time machine, But still, something inside me unknots. The world just feels so much more *right* with her in my arms. I want to stroke her back, but I don't know if that would be weird, so I just hold her securely until she's ready to talk more.

She gives one last sniff, loud and wet, then sits back. "Sorry for being such a girl."

"Don't worry, that's one of the main things I like about you."

She shoots me a weak smile. "Now what?"

"I don't know. Maybe we can . . . start over? Go back to being friends, like when we first met?" It's not really what I want, but I don't trust myself to give her more right now. I've just gotten traded to this team in what could be my biggest and most demanding season yet. I can't lose my focus.

Jane weighs my words. *Just friends.*

Last night's incredible kiss aside, there's no way she wants—or can trust—anything more intimate from me. As much as it hurts to accept it, that chapter of our lives is closed, and I'd rather have a platonic relationship with Jane than none at all. She owned all of my first times, and that will never change. But if friendship is all I'm going to get from her now, I'll have to try and accept that.

"I . . ." She takes a deep breath and wets her lips. "I think I can do that."

I place my big, warm palm directly over her flat stomach and rest it there. Neither of us speaks for a long time after that. This is huge for us. Just being in the same room and having her not wanting to kill me is a big deal. Her accepting my apology and agreeing to be friends is icing on the cake.

A little while later, our moment of contentment is interrupted by her stomach growling, and I laugh. "How about we kick off our new friendship with dinner?"

"Oh my God, food sounds amazing. I haven't eaten since those little pretzel packets on the plane." She grabs a tissue from the end table and blows her nose. "You mind if we order delivery? I'm too tired to go out into the world again."

I don't blame her. After a long day of playing and traveling, followed by history's most intense conversation, I'm pretty beat too. "Sure. What do you want?"

"Uh . . . I dunno, surprise me. There's some takeout menus on the fridge door." She gets off the couch. "I'm gonna go put on sweatpants. If I have to wear these clothes one more second, I might just climb out of my skin."

I snort, already dialing a Chinese restaurant. She soon reemerges, and while I order, she turns on the TV and starts browsing through her Netflix queue.

When I hang up the phone, she asks, "What kind of movies do you like?"

I shake my head with a smile. "No way. I picked what we eat, so you have to pick what we watch."

With a sly smirk, she flips to a pink-colored movie cover that screams chick flick.

I throw my hand over my eyes like I'm annoyed. "Aagh!"

Jane actually giggles at my melodramatic act. I haven't heard that sound in forever, and it eases something inside me.

She continues scrolling until we get to some sci-fi thriller-looking thing. Soon, we're flopped comfortably on the couch with our food. The atmosphere is finally casual.

I let out a sigh and unwind against the cushions. It's so nice to be around her again without all the tension from when I first got here.

Jane's a catch . . . a smart, tough, level-headed woman who gets football but isn't a groupie. She's also drop-dead gorgeous, but I try not to notice that.

All too well, I remember why I first fell for her, but I firmly remind myself that it's over between us. Considering how badly I blew it—both ten years ago and last night—this outcome is pretty damn lucky. Somehow, we're sitting together as friends, watching TV while shoveling spicy noodles into our faces, getting over a messy past I never thought we'd put behind us.

Even though she sits on the opposite end of the couch, a respectable platonic distance, I swear I can feel her warmth.

CHAPTER Eleven

Jane

It seems like everything in the world reminds me of Weston Chase.

Eating dinner at my parents' house later that week, I think about how Wes and I had our first kiss in this kitchen. Mom asks me to pass the pasta, and I wonder how many servings Wes would have to eat to be full. Dad brings up work, and I jump at any chance I get to bring up Wes's amazing work ethic. It seems like no matter what I do, I can't get him out of my head.

"Janie? Are you there?"

I snap out of another Wes-inspired fantasy and look up to find my parents staring wide-eyed at me.

"Yeah, yeah, sorry. What did you say?"

"I asked if you were feeling all right," Dad says. "You seem a little all over the place tonight. Work got you caught up?"

"Something like that," I say, twisting the last bit of pasta onto my fork. "But things are fine, Dad. I promise."

Better than fine, actually. Ever since Wes and I talked things through and cleared the air about what happened all those years ago, it feels like I've had ten years of weight lifted off my shoulders. An honest apology from him was exactly what I needed, and now that things are patched up, I've found myself letting go of my hesitation.

Maybe Wes really has left his douchebaggery in his teenage years, and something could work between us after all. He suggested we go back to being friends, but after the way he kissed me? A girl doesn't just forget about a kiss like that. And our texts all week have definitely erred on the side of flirty. There's no denying that.

A smirk tugs up my mouth as I wiggle my phone out of my back pocket and fire off a quick message.

`What are you up to tonight?`

Aside from dinner with my parents, I have no other plans for the evening. I wouldn't mind another one of those delicious back massages, especially if it ends in a steamy kiss like last time.

"Texting at the dinner table?" Mom scolds playfully. "I think that means you're doing dishes tonight."

Returning my phone to its rightful place in my pocket, I pop out of my chair and start gathering our dirty plates.

"Leave mine," Dad says, nodding at his plate. "I'm going in for another round of that salad. Only your mother could make salad taste that good."

He shoots Mom a wink, and she rolls her eyes, giggling. They're still so in love after all these years. I want a love like that.

My phone buzzes in my back pocket, which I can only hope means a response from Wes. Plates stacked high, I shuffle off to the sink, quickly dropping them in the soapy water to free my hands. My stomach flips at the message on my screen.

`Bouta be balls deep in a couple of jersey chasers, wbu?`

You've got to be kidding me. My stomach twists into a painful knot.

Is this what he had in mind when he said we should be friends? Him telling me about him fucking other girls? He hasn't changed at all since we broke up. In fact, he's gotten worse. How could I be so stupid?

I slam my phone onto the counter, the screen facing down, and grab the sponge. Might as well take my anger out on the pasta sauce encrusted on the dinner plates. Before I can start in on the first , my phone buzzes again. This time, it's a call.

What else could that jerk possibly have to add to that last crude comment?

I snatch my phone off the counter and hurry into the living room, out of my parents' earshot. I don't want Dad to hear me chewing out his precious quarterback.

"What?" I snap into the phone. There's a rumble of voices and electronic music in the background. Wes is with the team, and with the women who flock to them, no doubt.

"Jane, I'm so sorry," he yells over the noise. "That last text, I'm not the one who sent it. One of the other players saw I had a text from you, and thought it would be funny."

The tension in my chest releases. *Thank God.*

"Yeah, real funny," I mutter, my tone equal parts annoyed and relieved.

"What did you say? This place is too damn loud. Let me get somewhere quieter so I can hear you." The background noise fades as Wes distances himself from the crowd. "This any better?"

"Yeah, much better. Where are you?"

"At a bar downtown. Almost half the team is here, and somehow I'm the one who got stuck as designated driver. Lucky me, right?" I can practically hear him rolling his eyes through the phone. "Not that they need me. They're all going home with girls anyway. I'm thinking about just calling cabs for all of them and calling it a night."

"Going to bed early?" I say, testing the waters. I'd love to see him tonight, even briefly, but I don't want to get between him and his beauty rest, if that's his plan.

"Nah, I'm still wide awake. But I think my couch is calling my name. I'd love if you joined me, though. We could watch a movie, kill a bottle of red wine. I owe you a drink after that text you just got."

My head buzzes in giddy anticipation. He's choosing an evening curled up on the couch with me over the bar scene with his team. I can hardly believe it.

"Are you sure? I don't want to steal you from the guys." That's a thinly veiled lie. Of course I'd rather have him all to myself tonight, but I know team bonding is important, especially for a newer team member like Wes.

"Trust me, Jane," Wes says, his voice suddenly hushed and sincere. "I'd take a night in with you over any bar in this city."

My cheeks blaze with sudden heat. That's not the sort of thing you say to just a friend.

Which is what we agreed on, but I wonder if he really means it, or is just trying to go slow. We hash out the details, and I agree to head over to his place in an hour, enough time for me to wrap things up with my parents and for him to make sure all his drunk teammates are getting safely to their destinations.

After we hang up, I hurry back to the kitchen. I haven't forgotten about dish duty. While Mom scoops leftover pasta into plastic containers, I get to work scrubbing every inch of the dinner plates with the speed of a seasoned restaurant dishwasher.

Mom seems impressed. "Since when are you so domestic?" she asks, one eyebrow perked in curiosity.

I shrug. Since I got a hot date on the other side of this stack of dirty dishes.

My memory replays our hotel-room make-out session, and part of me wants to take the reins and initiate something more tonight. It's not like we haven't had sex before, and after ten years without sleeping with him, I'm definitely developing a craving for it. Maybe tonight is the night to make my move.

The second I set the last almost-clean plate into the dishwasher, Dad lets out a bear-sized yawn. It's barely eight o'clock. My parents are real party animals. But their early bedtime gives me an easy excuse me to hit the road, so I slip on my leather jacket and start the good-bye hugs, thanking them for dinner. Mom insists on sending enough leftovers home with me to feed a small army, a.k.a. the perfect amount of food for a football player. I'm sure Wes won't turn down chicken and pasta if I bring it over.

"Have a good night, Janie!" Dad calls as I dash out the door.

But if things go the way I want them to, "good" won't even begin to describe tonight.

• • •

Knowing that Wes could afford some crazy modern mansion with his NFL salary, it's even more endearing that he's chosen to live with a friend of his. Hauling my grocery bag of leftovers up the front steps, I can't help but smile. The boy I fell for all those years ago hasn't let his success and fame go to his head. Hot and humble. Talk about the whole package.

I buzz twice, listening to the pad of feet coming downstairs, the metallic sound of the door unlocking, and finally, the creak of the door swinging open, revealing a smile bright enough to light up the whole block.

"Hey, you made it."

I step through the door and Wes engulfs me in his arms, pulling me tight against him. My cheeks barely come up to his pecs, and for a second, I can hear his heartbeat speed up before he lets me go.

"Come on in. I'm out of wine, so I hope gin and

tonic is okay."

I'm secretly grateful for the change in drink menu. Drinking wine with Wes reminds me of the past. The last time we split a bottle of wine was the night before he left for college, and I want to leave the past in the past tonight.

"A gin and tonic sounds beyond perfect," I say as he leads me down the hall to the living room, gesturing for me to make myself comfortable before excusing himself to the kitchen to mix our drinks.

I set the bag of leftovers on the coffee table and run my fingers across the arm of one of the leather couches. My mood has improved so much since the last time I was here for the team pizza party. I remember practically using Alex as a human shield to avoid running into Wes.

"You plan to stay here long term?" I ask.

"Nah, probably not," Wes replies, his low, rumbling voice echoing in the kitchen. "Colin had a spare bedroom and let me move in since my transfer was so last minute. It was no big deal, since we lived together in college and everything. I figure I'll move into an apartment once the season's done. I'll have more time to look for places then."

He returns to the couch with a drink in each hand, each glass sporting a wedge of lime. He passes one to me and raises his own in a toast.

"But lucky for us, we've got the place to ourselves tonight."

Clink. I'll drink to that.

The gin and tonic goes down smoothly, and I can't help but think how good the lime will taste on Wes's mouth later. *One step at a time, Jane. We've barely agreed to be friends, and now I want to jump him.*

We sit beside each other on the couch, but the plastic grocery bag on the coffee table demands my attention first.

"You know what would be good with a gin and tonic? Pasta." I snatch up the grocery bag and hand it to Wes. He peeks in, and his jaw drops open when he sees the enormous amount of leftovers. "My mom cooked, not me. And I already ate, so those are all yours. Figured that's about enough for a late-night snack for you."

Wes gives me a thankful grin, then heads back toward the kitchen to reheat the food. I settle into the couch, sipping my drink as I enjoy the show of watching him leave. He's got on a baseball style T-shirt that accentuates those gorgeous back muscles in all the right ways.

I make quick work of my drink, emptying my glass by the time Wes sits next to me with his enormous serving of pasta.

"Another one?" he asks, nodding toward my glass.

I shake my head. I don't want him running in and out of the kitchen all night. I want him here, next to me.

"Well, here, feel free to have as much of mine as you want." He reaches over to swap my empty glass with his, letting his arm brush my thigh, which I can only hope is intentional.

"You'll have to send my compliments to the chef," he says after a few bites of pasta. "I've missed your mom's cooking. How is she? Good?"

I talk a bit about my evening as Wes finishes the plate of food and then sets the empty dish on the table. As I'm babbling about dinner with my parents, Wes drapes his arm across the back of the couch, comfortable in my proximity, or just plain comfortable. I'm not sure.

"Still can't believe I'm here—on this team,

back in Chicago. It's surreal."

He doesn't say it, but I think he also means he can't believe he's *here*, sitting with me. Part of me can't believe it either, but I'm not ready to talk about what this might or might not mean, so instead I steer the conversation toward football. It's always been a safe topic for us.

"You really did it." I gaze at him and smile.

He smiles back, but there's a tinge of sadness in it. Becoming a pro football player has always been his dream—his one-in-a-million dream. And it came true. But it hasn't been handed to him. He's earned every bit of it, devoting countless hours to honing his craft, perfecting his throwing arm, spending just as many hours in the gym as he does on the field. There have been sacrifices to get here. And I'm starting to understand that I was one of them. You don't get to this level by chance, and Wes has prioritized his life to arrive at this precise moment.

I remember watching the televised draft with my dad in our den a few years after Wes and I broke up. I tried to avoid all things football in the years following our breakup, but I couldn't *not* know if he was really going to make it to the big leagues. Some desperate, hidden part of me had to know.

When the announcer called his name and the team that had selected him, silent tears streamed down my cheeks. He looked happy, so fucking happy. A smile every bit as wide as the ones I used to be responsible for overtook his face. He made it. All the sacrifices and years of hard work paid off. All of his dreams came true while I had been home nursing a broken heart and an empty womb.

But something about the expression on his face now as he gazes down on me tells me that he's re-evaluating if it's all been worth it. That old saying "it's lonely at the top" pops into my brain and sticks. For all of his hard work and devotion, he has no one to share the happy moments with, no one to hold him and let him vent when things go to shit. Which they often do in this game.

Something in his eyes tells me that he knows he's missed out. Despite being one of the highest-paid players in the country, despite getting to play a game he loves for a living, he's alone. And lonely. And it's completely his own doing.

This is not me feeling bad for him. This is just me acknowledging how we arrived here.

Wes takes a deep breath and the tension between us falls away, even if that silent acknowledgment remains.

"Do you still love it?"

"The game?" he asks, his voice now sounding smoky.

I nod.

He thinks about this question for a long time. "The game, yes. All the other bullshit, the politics in this league, no."

Now it makes more sense why he wanted to come to the Hawks, to play under my father. Dad is known for being the straightest-shooting, say-what's-on-his-mind coach out there. You always know where you stand, he doesn't leave you wondering if you might get cut or traded. He's open from the word *go*, and highly respected. Or maybe it was just that Wes wanted his shot at redemption—a shot with me, but that's not something I want to ponder right now.

We're just friends. But when I meet Wes's dark gaze, being friends is the last thing on my mind. The truth is he's so freaking sexy, and no man has ever gotten me hot the way he does.

Without taking his gaze off me, he moves closer. One arm is still on the back of the couch, pulled around my shoulders, and his other hand moves to my knee, one finger innocently touching the hem of my skirt.

Fuck. I stop midsentence, biting down on my lower lip.

Wes shakes his head, letting a quick breath of air out of his nose in a muted laugh. “That drives me nuts, you know that?”

Confused, I cock my head. “What does?”

“When you bite your lip like that.” He runs his finger along the hem of my skirt, then to the top of my thigh. “Drives me absolutely fucking crazy.”

My breath catches in the back of my throat. “Crazy bad or crazy good?”

Keeping his fingers on my knee, Wes pulls his arm from behind my shoulders and softly grips the nape of my neck, pulling me fiercely against him, and presses his mouth softly against mine in a slow kiss.

My heartbeat riots in my chest the second his lips meet mine. They’re soft, yet demanding and I answer his kiss, opening my mouth and letting his tongue touch mine. He tastes like gin and lime and heartbreak, and so many things I won’t let myself think about right now. When he pulls back, it’s his turn to bite my lip, tugging on it gently with his teeth.

"In case that didn't answer your question," Wes murmurs, his lips traveling to my neck, working their way up to whisper in my ear. "Crazy good."

When his lips meet mine again, I push gently against his chest, letting him ease onto his back as I move to his lap and wrap my knees around his hips, letting my tongue playfully explore his mouth. His kisses unlock some secret part of me, and I whimper, tangling my hands in his short hair, using it to tug him even closer. Wes lets out a low groan that rumbles in his chest and rocks his hips against mine in time with his kissing, and I can feel how hard he is beneath me.

Dear God . . .

The thought of his beautiful cock just a few layers of fabric beneath me makes the lace of my underwear go damp.

Shit. I know we agreed to be just friends, but here, drowning in him and his masculinity, it seems like the most futile agreement in the world.

"Maybe you should show me your bedroom," I whisper between the kisses I'm trailing down his neck.

He lets out a low hum of agreement, then pauses, momentarily releasing his grip on my shirt. "I want to make sure you're sure about this, though."

He's so gentle and sincere, I almost forget that I'm currently straddling him.

"Don't get me wrong," he says, "I've wanted you in my bed since the moment you walked in. But I'm just as happy watching a movie out here. We don't have to do anything you're not comfortable with."

My mouth twitches into a coy smile as I squeeze my thighs tight against Wes's body, cupping his cheeks in my palms and planting a slow, sweet kiss on his mouth.

"Wes, you're so sweet. Thank you. But I'm more comfortable with you than I've ever been with anyone else. And I'd be even more comfortable on a bed instead of a couch."

His hungry gaze meets mine, and in one fell swoop, he's up on his feet, scooping me off of him and into his arms, almost knocking his empty plate off the coffee table in the process.

A laugh bubbles out of me, but Wes doesn't flinch. It seems nothing can distract him from his task—that task being me. He leans in and nips at my earlobe in retaliation, sending a jolt of electricity between my thighs.

"I'll get it later," he mutters into my ear. "Besides, no offense to your mom's cooking, but you taste way better."

Oh.

My feet dangle off the edge of Wes's king-size bed, making me feel even smaller than I usually do around him. As his mouth makes its way back to mine, he pushes my skirt up to my hips and out of his way, the rough skin of his hands palming my ass while his mouth ventures down my neck, along my collarbone, lingering over my breasts. His hot breath makes my nipples harden, pushing up against the cups of my bra.

Our mouths meet again in a hungry kiss, and a desperate groan escapes my throat. Like two sides of a magnet, we were drawn together. In this moment, I believe everything I've ever heard about muscle memory, because that's what this is. There's no awkward fumbling, no need to go slow and learn what the other likes. We fit together like a lock and key.

And suddenly I need more. I'm out of my white V-neck in seconds.

"Jesus, Jane," Wes whispers, his gaze dropping to my breasts.

He's looking at me with such worshipful desire, it makes my insides turn molten. Then his mouth returns to my breasts, kissing along the pale lace of my bra, which he unclasps with ease and tosses to the floor. He circles each stiff pink nipple with his thumb, making my body tremble under his touch.

Good God, he remembers exactly how to turn me on. I may have the body of a grown woman now, but it's just as weak to his touch as it was a decade ago. Every muscle clenches and contracts as he takes my right nipple in his lips, sucking, then nipping gently, pulling a gasp out of me.

He glances up at me with a look of satisfaction. "You haven't changed one bit," he whispers, flicking my nipple with his tongue. "And I fucking love it."

He keeps this up, sucking and flicking and nipping as he bunches my skirt all the way up and around my waist, the lace of my panties fully exposed. One teasing finger runs over the fabric, grazing my clit, and I shudder.

I'm so wet, so ready. I need him to touch me.

He takes my mouth in his and slowly begins

stroking, circling my clit from outside my panties, and I moan into his mouth. His touch is so familiar, but he was never this much of a tease before. I think I like it.

Finally, enough teasing. Pulling the wet, lacy fabric to the side, Wes plunges his middle finger deep into me and I moan again, curving my hips against his hand as he slides in and out. It's been so long since anyone has been inside me. As he adds a second finger, I can tell I'm tight.

If my memory of his cock serves me right, we might have to work our way up to that.

My pulse quickens as I grind against the curl of Wes's fingers, snug inside me, hitting all the right spots. I'm already panting, nearing climax from his fingers alone, when Wes drops to his knees and takes my clit between his lips.

Holy shit.

His mouth is gentle, his fingers persistent, and it doesn't take more than a minute for me to wind all the way up and then come completely loose, climaxing onto his fingers. He parts me with his tongue, tasting me as I shudder, then kisses my inner thigh and releases my underwear back to its rightful position.

"Holy shit." I sigh, exasperated. "I didn't think it was possible, but you've somehow gotten even better at that."

Wes smiles and rises to his feet beside the bed, his erect cock jutting out in front of him, pressing insistently against his jeans. I love knowing that tasting me got him so aroused.

Leaning over me, Wes plants his lips on mine and kisses the last bit of breath out of me, then stands up, heading toward his closet.

"Um, where are you going?"

He pivots, giving me a confused look. "To put on my pajamas so we can go to bed. Is that okay with you?"

I fold my arms over my chest, scrunching my eyebrows. "Before I get to return the favor?"

Wes chuckles and rubs the back of his neck with one hand, his biceps flexing in that baseball tee as he does. God, he's gorgeous.

"You don't have to do that, Jane. I don't want you to feel obligated to return the favor. Plus, not to brag, but it seems like I wore you out quite a bit just now."

I raise my eyebrows at him, accepting the challenge, and beckon him back to the bed with one finger.

"Well, I'm not going to say no to that," he says, peeling off his shirt to reveal those perfectly chiseled abs, just as gorgeous as they were that day in the locker room.

But this time, I don't have to pretend not to stare. As he leans over the bed to kiss me, I can't resist running my fingers over them, which gets a smile out of him.

"You're practically photoshopped, you know that, right?" I tease.

"I just work really hard." He shrugs, hot and humble once again.

I paint each individual ab with my tongue until my mouth is in line with the chiseled *V* poking out of his dark-wash jeans. I unbutton his pants, freeing his erection.

Yup, my memory serves me correctly, all right. He's huge. But I've done this before, and I can't wait to do it again.

I let Wes take my place on the edge of the bed as I drop to my knees, running a finger down the thick vein in his shaft. He lets out a wavering exhale.

Good. I remember just as much about getting him going as he does for me.

He weaves his fingers through my hair as I take his full length in my mouth, slowly at first, then quicker and quicker, running my tongue along his shaft as I work him over.

"Shiiit. Goddamn, Jane."

Wes's moan is like music to me, like the radio playing a song I had long forgotten about and I still know every word. As his grip tightens on my hair, I move faster and faster, letting him slide down my throat.

I bring one hand around his shaft, pumping him in my fist as my mouth glides up and down.

His ab muscles tighten and clench, and he makes a low hum of approval in his throat. "Oh, fuck yes."

When his breathing quickens, I gaze up at him with the best *fuck me* eyes I can manage. One look, and he tips over the edge, finishing in the back of my throat. I swallow it and ease him out of my mouth, then plant one final kiss on the head of his cock. Just like I always used to do.

“Wow. I just . . . Thank you.”

Wes is speechless. He lifts me onto his lap and presses a grateful kiss against my lips, which says it all. And I kiss him back. Over and over and over.

We collapse onto his bed, taking turns pressing grateful kisses onto each other’s lips, cheeks, noses, ears. I want to kiss every inch of him. When we’re too tired to kiss anymore, he pulls me into the crook of his arm.

“God, Jane.” He sighs sleepily, squeezing me tight against him. “I never should have let you go.”

CHAPTER *Twelve*

Weston

I can still smell Jane on my pillow. I close my eyes and take a deep breath of the scents of her shampoo, her sweat, her desire . . . the desire I still can't believe she shared with me.

I never thought she'd want to touch me again—and damn, *how* she touched me. I can still feel the burning touch of her hands and mouth on my skin. Despite all the fun we just had, my cock threatens to stir again.

I feel for my phone on the nightstand and text her.

`Let me know when you're home.`

Eighteen minutes later—almost exactly how long it takes to get from my place to hers—she replies.

I'm here. You worried about me?

Just wanted to make sure you got back okay.

I consider for a moment, then decide I don't care about playing it cool.

And one last chance to say good night.

You'll see me again in less than twelve hours.

I can picture Jane rolling her eyes, a smile tugging at the corners of her mouth.

I know. Still wanted to say it.

Thank you. :) Now go to sleep or you'll be tired for practice tomorrow.

She's not asleep either, yet she's lecturing me like the good little manager she is.

I put down my phone and roll over onto my back, stacking my hands behind my head. I'm too happy to actually do what she said. Instead, I want to keep replaying the evening and make sure I remember every detail. Her silky skin and hair, her cries of pleasure, the way she trembled against me . . .

Somehow, without knowing when, I drift off to warm, horny thoughts of Jane.

• • •

There's a spring in my step all the next morning. Even during my bicep curls, which is usually the most boring part of my strength-training routine, I find myself humming along to the pop radio station piped into the weight room.

"You're cheerful today," Colin remarks from the neighboring leg-press machine.

I quickly wipe off the smile I didn't even known

I was wearing. "I am? Didn't notice."

I'm sure he just meant it as an idle comment, but the last thing I need is to start rumors flying. Jane is my coach's daughter, and also technically one of my bosses.

Plus, I'm still not sure exactly what it is we're doing. I'm definitely down for more action, but the fact that we messed around once doesn't tell me anything about her feelings or plans. And I really have no idea where I stand with her.

"He's what?" Alex stops on his way past us.

God dammit. We just had to get his attention, didn't we.

"In a good mood," Colin says.

"It's nothing." I grunt, wishing Colin wouldn't be quite so helpful all the time.

"Well, now I *know* it's something," Alex says. "And . . . hey, why are you here?"

I frown at him in confusion. "Where the hell else would I be?"

"Last night at the bar, when you ditched us, you said you were going home because you didn't feel well. But here you are, working out like normal."

"Must've been a twenty-four-hour flu kind of bug," Colin says, and I silently thank him for his loyalty.

Alex lifts his eyebrows in a pointed *oh, come on* look. "Do you seriously believe that? I'm betting he ran off to meet a girl. It'd explain why he's in such a good mood this morning."

Colin looks skeptical, but now I'm not sure if that look is directed at me or Alex. "Naw . . . really? You think so?"

I growl under my breath. "Dammit, you're supposed to be on my side."

Colin chuckles. "Relax, man, we're just messing with you."

I'm still a few reps away from finishing my last set, but I stand up and push past Alex anyway. "Excuse me."

"You mad, bro?" Alex is smirking.

"I will be if you don't move your ass so I can rack my weights."

Coach Royce saves me by sticking his head into the room. "Hit the showers, boys, and be quick about it. Team meeting starts in twenty minutes."

Players start wrapping up, wiping down their benches and going through their cooldown routines.

I'm in such a hurry to escape everyone bugging me that I'm one of the first players out of the shower and into the meeting room. Coach Royce and Mr. Flores are already there . . . and so is Jane, sitting at the side of the room. She's wearing olive slacks, a white button-up blouse, and brown flats.

It's a perfectly professional outfit, but I can't stop staring, and I know it's because of the woman wearing it. She looks so beautifully put together, in control, in her element.

Though it doesn't help that her slacks cling, revealing the outline of her legs. Just that suggestion of shape is enough to make me think about tracing those curves with my hands, caressing her calves, kissing my way up to her thighs and beyond.

Coach Royce's voice yanks me out of my increasingly filthy thoughts. "I have some new ideas about the upcoming Swashbucklers game."

I blink, looking around to see that everyone else is seated. The meeting has started, and I barely noticed.

Coach launches straight into his explanation.

His plan of attack and the reasons behind it are solid. More than solid—downright brilliant. But Jane crosses one leg over the other, the round swell of her hip and butt straining against the fabric of her slacks, and my gaze slides right back to her like it's magnetized.

"So if we use the new formation here . . ."

Shit, I wasn't paying attention. I try to focus on the complicated play diagram Coach is drawing on the whiteboard. Not the way Jane twirls her gorgeous hair around her finger while taking notes. Not Jane chewing her full, pink lower lip in concentration. Nope, not at all interested in the woman who's dominated my thoughts since I got here, and who I just spent last night getting better acquainted with.

". . . which puts us in a short-yardage situation, perfect for the jumbo we've been drilling. Then all we have to do is . . ."

Why didn't I hear the first part of that sentence? I swear to God, I was listening that time.

Wait, was Jane looking at me just now? I sneak a glance, and my eyes meet hers with an almost physical jolt of electricity.

Has she been thinking about me? Is she smiling

or is it just my wishful imagination? Does she want me as badly as I want her?

All the memories of last night are running wild through my brain. God, I wish we could get out of here and—

Coach Royce barks, "Chase!"

I almost jump out of my seat. "Y-yes, sir?"

"As amazing as my daughter is, she's not the one who's gonna stop your ass from getting sacked this Sunday."

I sit up ramrod straight and try to look serious. Jane intently examines the wall in the opposite direction, her cheeks pinkening. I might be imagining it, but I think Coach Royce's mouth twitches.

"Do I need to remind you what the Cobras did to us last week?" he asks.

My stomach twists a little. "No, sir."

He nods sharply. "Good. Because there's a lot riding on this next game. As I was saying . . ." He dives back into his analysis of the Swashbucklers' players and tactics.

Keeping my focus on Coach Royce and off his daughter is still borderline impossible. But Jane is taking notes . . . the perfect excuse to go find her later and talk privately. Maybe even steal a kiss or five.

• • •

It's just past midnight on Saturday, and I'm pacing my hotel room in my boxers, hopelessly awake. The more I think about the game tomorrow, the more restless I feel. I should find something boring on TV to lull me to sleep, but nothing holds my interest enough to even calm me down.

On a whim, I grab my phone and text Jane, not really expecting an answer at such a late hour.

Can't sleep.

To my pleasant surprise, my phone lights up with a reply just a couple of minutes later.

Me neither. I'm just lying in bed, bored out of my mind.

A smile tugs at my mouth.

Oh? Maybe I should come keep you

company.

She'll probably just call me a horndog, but our little teasing games are a lot more fun than tying myself in anxious knots all night.

My playful mood heats up at her reply.

Maybe I should let you.

Keep talking like that and you're going to get me in trouble.

ME get YOU in trouble? In high school, you were always the one convincing me to play hooky and do crazy shit.

Maybe so, but remember our last team meeting?

Excuse you? I was minding my own business, thanks. :P

`You were wearing those tight slacks. Biting your lip and twirling your hair . . . you know, those cute habits you always do when you're thinking hard.`

`I didn't realize any of those things were illegal.`

`Illegal, no. Irresistible, yes.`

She doesn't respond. Just as I start wondering if I offended her somehow, someone knocks on my door. I look through the peephole and grin at the sight of a pajama-clad Jane.

The instant I open up, she surges into me with a fiery kiss. Every nerve in my body sparks to life. I slam the door shut and match her. Our mouths devour each other as she explores the hard muscle of my chest and back, and I let my hands wander over her tempting curves.

When I start fumbling with her pajama top's buttons, she answers with a throaty noise and eager hands tugging at my waistband. She cups my bulge firmly, and I groan. In less than a minute, she's gotten me so maddeningly hard, so greedy for more.

We stumble toward the bed, tearing at each other's clothes, but we only make it as far as the armchair. I push her to sit down and I kneel, kissing and biting at her bared breasts until I can tug off her pajama shorts and panties. Then I bury my face between her thighs and relish her loud gasp.

She smells so good and tastes even better, sweet with slick arousal. My cock aches, but all I can think about is making her come. She bucks and whimpers as I lash my tongue against her swollen bud.

My tongue works faster, and I tease two fingers against her opening until she squirms with impatience, then I slip them inside and find the spot that makes her whimper. I remember what she liked best so long ago and discover new ways, new spots that make her cry out.

I focus on her body so she can guide me by her ragged panting, the twitches of her fingers tangled in my hair, her legs locked around my face and shoulders. A trembling that intensifies to full-body quaking as I push her higher, closer . . .

With a moan, she arches up, grinding hard into

my face. Her whole pussy pulsates against my mouth, nose, and chin, clenching around the two fingers still inside her. I keep going until she rides out the waves of her climax and shudders with overstimulation.

I let her go, and she slumps back with a far-away look in her eyes.

"That was . . . intense." Her voice is still husky with pleasure.

It was for me too. I take a deep breath and look up at her, admiring her flushed cheeks, sex-wild hair, and sprawled, relaxed posture. Nothing is better than seeing that buzzed, satiated expression and knowing I was the one who put it there.

"Wipe that smirk off your face," she murmurs, smiling a little herself, "and tell me how you want me."

I reach down and give my cock a warning squeeze, but I shake my head. "I'm okay."

She blinks. "Wes. You don't want anything in return?" Her gaze flicks down to the straining evidence of my desire.

I stand up, a little light-headed. "I do, but I also don't want to mess with my focus for tomorrow's game."

"That old superstition?" She giggles. "Sex before a game doesn't really drain your 'manly energy,' you know." She curls her fingers in scare quotes as she says it. "Your football talent isn't hidden in your balls."

I laugh aloud. "Trust me . . ." I lean down to give her a good-night peck on the forehead. "Touching you is more than enough."

Her smile is sweet, almost shy. "If you say so. Can I at least . . . you want one more kiss, y'know, for good luck?"

"Like I could say no to that." I pull her to her feet and savor everything she offers.

Chapter Thirteen

Jane

The two most beautiful words in all of professional football: bye week, a.k.a. the one week of the season where our team doesn't have a game on the schedule, a.k.a. sweet freedom. No traveling, drastically reduced hours on the practice field, and a chance for every player, trainer, manager, and coach to catch their breath and enjoy a little sanity in the midst of an otherwise insane season.

Yes, I love my job more than any sane person should, but that doesn't mean I don't need a break every once in a while. In past years, I've spent the entirety of this week plopped on my couch, interacting exclusively with the Thai food delivery guy and the host of whatever game show I'm binge-watching.

But this year is different. I'm trading in my extra-large order of pad Thai for an apple orchard date with Wes, and if things go the way I hope they will, an evening with him back at my place. The only way I'll be spending any time on my couch tonight is if he and I don't make it to the bedroom.

I don't want to assume that we'll have sex tonight, but based on the past few evenings Wes and I have spent together, I'm liking my odds. And truth be told, I haven't been able to get the feel of his kiss out of my head, or the taste of the rest of him, for that matter. It's like I have the world's biggest sweet tooth, and Wes is made of pure sugar. The cravings are constant and relentless.

When I see Wes pull to a stop outside my building, I don't give him the chance to come up. I race downstairs and meet him on the curb before he's even made it to the door.

"Hey." He smiles.

"Hi." I grin back at him. Jeez, I feel a little light-headed in his presence. My belly tightens, and my heart starts to pound faster.

The crisp early October air nips at my cheeks as I swing open the passenger door and climb into his rental car. Wes climbs in beside me, and when he starts it up, the thumping beats of a rap song pump over the speakers. I recognize it as the same song we sang along to on the drive back from Walmart.

Well played, Chase.

"Nice song choice," I say over the deep thumping bass.

He turns the volume down a few notches, his eyes doing a quick once-over of my legs in these skintight black jeans. "Damn. You look amazing."

That's the idea, big boy.

My cheeks flush, and I fist my fingers around the sleeves of my flannel shirt to keep from reaching over and grabbing him right here in broad daylight.

"Thanks," I squeak, trying to conceal my blushing cheeks behind a curtain of my hair. As he drives out of the parking lot, I fight off the urge to yell "Stop the car!" and forego the date altogether in favor of a full day in the bedroom.

Patience, Jane. You're the one who suggested the apple orchard in the first place.

The memory of our bowling date flits through my memory and I relax, letting my sex drive temporarily take a back seat. I might as well enjoy the ride before I, well, enjoy the *ride*.

The orchard is just a short drive outside of the city limits, and since it's a Tuesday afternoon, I can count the number of cars in the gravel parking lot on one hand.

"Looks like we've practically got the place to ourselves," Wes says as he shifts the car into park.

The only person in sight is the woman manning the entrance booth, standing next to a stack of big white buckets waiting to be filled with apples. Clearly, it's been a slow day—she's flipping lazily through the pages of a celebrity gossip magazine, and only looks up when Wes clears his throat to get her attention.

"Can we get two buckets, please?"

He pulls a twenty out of his wallet and the woman silently accepts it, gesturing to the stack of plastic buckets to indicate we should help ourselves. I was kind of expecting her to recognize Wes from the Hawks like the bowling-shoe guy did, but if she does, she shows no sign of it.

Once we've taken our buckets, she points us toward the orchard and returns to her magazine. Not a big football fan, I guess.

"Shall we?" Wes offers me his free hand and I eagerly take it, lacing my fingers tightly with his.

Even if there's no one around to see, his willingness to hold my hand in public makes me giddy. His thumb strokes my knuckles as we weave through the rows and rows of apple trees, scouting out the reddest and ripest fruit. We release our grip when we agree on a particularly good tree, and set our buckets on the ground. He plucks apples from the higher branches while I take care of the lower ones.

"The best ones are always high up," he says, tossing an apple into his half-full bucket. "All the good ones are still up there because hardly anybody can reach 'em."

I roll my eyes, snapping an apple off of a low branch. "That's a load of shit. The high-up ones are exactly the same as the low ones."

Wes gives me an *oh, really?* look and immediately sets out to prove his point. He surveys the nearby trees until he spots an especially tall one and grabs a bright red apple from the highest branch. He shrugs his eyebrows at me as he chomps down on the apple, making half of it disappear in just one bite.

"Mmm, try this." He holds what's left of the apple in front of my mouth so I can take a bite.

I do, my eyes on his as I bite down. I can't deny that he's right. It's so juicy, the perfect amount of sweet.

A dribble of juice escapes from the corner of my mouth, and Wes takes it as an opportunity. He cups my chin in his hand and leans down, kissing the skin where the apple juice trailed out, playfully lapping it up.

Holy fuck. So much for putting my sex drive in the back seat.

"Yum. Tastes good." He licks his lips and gives me a squinty smile. Somehow, I don't think he's talking about the fruit.

When he takes another slow, deliberate bite of the apple, I desperately wish that apple and I could trade places. There's no one around, and I'm half tempted to sneak behind an especially big tree and let him fuck me here and now, but that's a recipe for a tabloid scandal neither of us wants to be a part of.

I need to get that tempting mouth back to my place, stat. So I start grabbing apples, any apples, off the trees at twice the pace, using little to no discretion in my choosing.

"Whoa, you in a hurry?" he asks with a knowing chuckle.

I look at him over my shoulder as I empty a whole branch of apples into my bucket, filling it to the brim.

"Looks like I'm all done." I shrug. "Better head home."

He chuckles and raises an eyebrow at me, calling my bluff, but I've never been more serious.

In a moment of bold flirtatiousness, I pick up my bucket and Wes's and strut past him toward the parking lot, making sure to swing my hips a little extra so he gets a good view of my ass in these skintight jeans. If he's going to tempt me with a kiss like that, I'm going to tempt him right back.

"All right, all right, wait up," he calls, jogging to catch up with me and wrapping his arm snugly around my shoulders.

His touch is familiar, but it still sends a tingle of electricity shooting through me. Why is it that every touch feels so natural while still packing the excitement of the first? I don't understand it, but I hope it never wears off.

After Wes and I unload our bounty of apples into the back seat of his rental car, we swing into the farm stand to pick up a box of cinnamon doughnuts, which I crack open before we've even pulled out of the gravel parking lot. We make it most of the way home on back roads, but once we hit the city limits, it's nothing but red lights.

Shit. Like this car ride wasn't testing my patience already. Watching Wes's long, thick fingers drum against the steering wheel is practically torture. The thought sends my head spinning.

When we hit a particularly long red light right before the turn onto my street, I offer Wes the doughnut box, trying to distract myself.

"Any rules as to which doughnuts taste the best?"

"I'm actually kind of craving something else." Wes turns to me, his gaze running down my legs again before he shifts his attention back to the road.

Fuck.

"Well, maybe this will tide you over," I say, offering him a bite of a doughnut that I hold in front of his mouth.

I have to distract myself or I'm going to lose it.

I want him. Now. And based on the speed at which he's taking the turn onto my street, he's not feeling very patient either.

The car glides into a parking spot outside my building, and Wes shifts into park. I'm still holding up the doughnut when he turns to me with a deliciously intense stare.

"Looks good enough to eat."

Holy fuck. He's not looking at the doughnut. My mouth falls open, but Wes just smirks, gesturing for me to put the doughnut back in the box.

"Save it till we're in your place, okay?"

Oh, there's a lot I've been saving for then, Wes.

I do everything I can to keep my cool as we make our way to my floor, doughnuts and buckets of apples in hand. I can feel Wes's stare tracing my curves as I turn the key and he follows me into the kitchen.

He stops to set the buckets on the kitchen counter, but this box of doughnuts and I are on a mission, heading straight for the bedroom. I can hear him snickering from the kitchen as I take a seat on my bed, crossing my legs so that the box of doughnuts rests comfortably in my lap. I'm already three or four bites in when he strolls up and leans on the door frame to admire the view.

"Between you and those doughnuts, I feel like I'm looking at a three-course meal," he murmurs.

My cheeks go hot, surely turning bright red.

"But I prefer you over doughnuts," he says, and without missing a beat, his lips are on mine, his tongue exploring my mouth, his widespread fingers clutching my ass.

I've been waiting all day for this, and it's still better than anything I could have dreamed up.

Wes moves the box of doughnuts onto my bedside table, his mouth not straying from mine for a second, and I slide into his lap, wrapping my legs around his waist.

His mouth moves to my ear, trailing quick, passionate kisses down my jawline as his nimble fingers pop open each button of my flannel shirt, exposing my lacy black bra. He lets out a low hum of approval as he traces the cup of my bra with the pads of his fingers. Just the slightest touch is enough for my nipples to harden in arousal.

Fuck. I'm putty in his calloused hands.

He unclasps my bra and it tumbles off, giving him full rein over my tight pink nipples. He pinches them softly between his fingers, rolling them around with his thumbs, and I inhale sharply. As his fingers pinch and tease, my thighs squeeze tightly against him, pressure building inside me in anticipation.

Wes slips my flannel off my shoulders and casts it aside before lifting me off his lap, standing us both up. He peels off his own shirt, revealing those perfect abs before shifting his attention to my jeans.

"I can't take my eyes off your legs in these." He sighs, hooking his thumbs into my waistband.

With one firm tug, the button pops open, and I can't hold back my giggles as Wes helps me shimmy these skintight pants off, my lacy black thong going with them. He holds my hand like a coachman helping a princess out of a carriage as I step out of the clingy black fabric.

"God, you are gorgeous," he growls into my ear as he pulls me against him, palming my ass with one hand as the other circles my clit.

I shudder and groan, holding tight to his shoulders as he slides his middle finger into me. Fuck, I didn't realize how wet I was. My groans grow louder and louder as he adds a second finger, curving them both and sliding them faster and faster, in and out of my wetness.

I can't do this anymore. I need to fuck him now. I greedily reach for the button of his jeans, but he stops me, catching my hand in his.

"Time out. I want to be sure you're totally okay with this. And whatever this is."

His eyes are serious but compassionate, that perfect combination of intensity and kindness that drew me to him in the first place. It's like he has a magnetic force about him that pulled me in the day I met him and never let me go.

"Yes, I'm okay with it. More than okay. It's all I've been able to think about."

"You and me both." He gently tucks a strand of my hair behind my ear, his fingers lingering on the curve of my jaw. How can a professional quarterback be so gentle? "I just want to be respectful of your limits," he murmurs.

I smile softly, shaking my head. "No limits, Wes," I whisper. "I want you. All of you."

I reach for the button of his jeans again, and this time, he doesn't stop me. Once I've unbuttoned and unzipped them, his erection springs free as I slide the worn denim to the floor, giving his cock one long lick on my way back up, which makes him groan.

"Are you ready?" he asks, sliding his fingers back into me. "You're so wet for me."

"Yes."

I moan, throwing my head back as his fingers quicken within me again. It's practically heaven. I can hardly believe it's about to get better. Wes reaches for his jeans on the floor and pulls a square foil packet from the pocket.

"Oh, so you came prepared?" I say playfully, taking a seat on the bed. "Were you expecting this to happen?"

He strolls over to me, takes the small of my back in his palm, and lays me back onto the bed with a long, tender kiss.

"Can you blame me for being hopeful?" He tears into the package and rolls on the condom, then brings his knees to either side of me. "You okay?" he asks one more time.

I nod, wide-eyed and eager. I've been ready since I laid eyes on him in the locker room. He flexes his hips and all at once, he sinks his full length into me.

Holy shit. I arch my back, curving myself to fit against him, trembling as he hits deeper within me than I thought was even possible. It's been ten long years since he's been inside me, and back then, I remember thinking that it was good, that he was good. But I had nothing to compare it to.

Now, I can say with full certainty that "good" doesn't even begin to describe Weston Chase.

CHAPTER Fourteen

Weston

"Wes . . . more, oh God, Wes!" Jane pants, writhing beneath me.

I groan, my jaw clenched. I'm so close, and hearing her mewl my name doesn't help. I bury my face in the crook of her neck, nipping and licking, resisting the urge to suck a mark of ownership into her soft skin.

"Oh, oh fuck, don't stop, I'm . . ."

She gasps, and her eyes clench shut as she arches up, her hips straining to meet my thrusts and grind hard against me. All of her tightens—her hands on my shoulders, her thighs tense and her calves locked around my back, her pussy gripping my cock in spasming waves.

Helpless, I crush our mouths together and tumble over the edge after her.

Even after the overwhelming pleasure finally ebbs away, we stay entwined, her legs resting against my sides, my arms braced on either side of her head. Her still-quick breaths fan over my cheek and tickle ever so slightly.

Her deep blue eyes open, slow and heavy-lidded, to meet mine. Her lips curve subtly—and oh, God, I'm paralyzed. I need that sweet, secret smile. Need *her*, all to myself, every single day and night.

Jane breaks my paralysis by scooting toward the headboard to sit up.

Still thrown by that intense wash of feeling, I turn away from her and busy myself with pulling off the condom and tossing it in the trash. I move up next to her.

She chuckles, gazing at me with a smile. "You last a lot longer than you did in high school."

"You did not just say that to me." I tug her closer, the mood lightening to something more playful.

But to my surprise, Jane rests her head on my shoulder and lets out a deep sigh. Her body is still hot from exertion, slightly sticky with sweat, and very, very naked.

I like it a little too much.

We rest together like that for a while, comfortably lying in bed together. I cover us with a sheet and pull her close. Even with all our history, it never used to be like this. There was never time for post-sex cuddles or lounging naked in bed together. There was plenty of exploring and sneaking around, but it had all been under the watchful eye of her father, who demanded that Jane be returned every night by her ten o'clock curfew. This is . . . nice. Comfortable. I enjoy the feel of her warm skin on mine, and trail my knuckles along her arm.

"How's practice going?" she asks. "I haven't gotten a chance to drop by the field lately."

I noticed, but she doesn't need to know how keenly I've been aware of her absence. "Your father's been riding our asses into the turf. It's like the Swashbucklers crushed us instead of the other way around."

"Yep, that's Dad for you," she says. "Never satisfied, always pushing for more."

I grin at her. "Just like his daughter."

"You're disgusting." But she's laughing, and so

am I.

"Hey, I was talking about being a workaholic. You and your dirty mind were the one who made it about sex." I give her an innocent look.

"Don't even try to pretend you're not a pervert. And who are you to tell me to chill out, Mr. First-on-the-Field-Every-Morning?" Her smirk is challenging.

I search my mind for something that qualifies as trash talk but won't actually get me thrown out the window. "I don't know. If I'm the pervert, why were you so wet for me?"

"I was just picturing Ryan Gosling's face while you were inside me."

A short bark of laughter is my only response. God, this girl . . .

We trade a few more playful barbs before lapsing into silence. She's still leaning against me, and I'm glad for it. I want to put my arm around her, stroke her hair, kiss her again . . .

So, why don't I?

I'm suddenly self-conscious, which is ridiculous. Ten minutes ago, I was inside her, and now I'm wondering if a casual touch is okay?

But I know that my desire to hold her isn't casual. Platonic friends don't feel a surge of need and passion and tenderness every time they look at each other. They don't have to work so hard to remind themselves to keep their distance, or twinge somewhere deep inside when they succeed. And they don't struggle with the uncertainty that's creeping up on me now. The sense that I'm playing with fire flares up inside of me.

This silence isn't comfortable anymore, but I can't think of anything else to say. I glance at the clock. Shit, it's almost midnight. It's always so easy to lose track of time with Jane, especially in bed. We should really get some sleep, or tomorrow will suck royally.

But I hesitate to just flop down and start snoring—she hasn't invited me to stay the night. She'd probably say yes if I asked, but that's precisely why I'm reluctant to. I wouldn't know if she actually wanted me next to her, or if she was just politely accommodating me.

I clear my throat. "Uh . . . well, I guess I'll get going now." I sit up and start pulling my pants back on.

She blinks but doesn't stop me. "Oh, okay. Sure. See you at work."

When I'm dressed, she walks me to the door. I still can't read her expression. I can tell she's tired, of course, and she seems content, but is that truth or wishful thinking? Is she sad or relieved to see me go?

With a wave that hopefully isn't too awkward, I step out and close the door behind me. I can't force myself to walk away until the dead bolt clicks into the lock.

On the drive home, I wonder where this weird atmosphere came from all of a sudden.

Sleeping with Jane didn't feel wrong—how could it ever? But I can't shake the sense that I made a mistake. Maybe it wasn't smart to jump into bed with her so soon . . . or possibly at all. Maybe some things can never truly be laid to rest, no matter how much work you put into them. Is our past just too messy to overcome?

I shake my head. Why am I getting so worked up over this? I don't even know if she's interested in dating in the first place. For that matter, am I? We're both married to our careers, and between Jane and Trista, I clearly have a terrible track record with relationships. I should just chill out and let things take their course. There's no reason to get so confused and start overanalyzing every tiny detail.

So, why can't I drag my brain away from her? From the *us* that doesn't even exist?

I pull into the driveway at Colin's house, park, and go in to get ready for bed, still puzzling over where Jane and I are heading.

• • •

Coach Royce blows his whistle and shouts, "All right, that's enough for now. Take five, boys. But stay ready for more . . . I'll be back soon." He starts across the field to more closely supervise the defensive team's agility drills.

I gratefully retreat to the bench, along with the rest of the offensive players, and gulp down a few swigs of cold water. I take off my helmet, letting the breeze cool my sweaty hair.

"You look wrecked."

I glance up to see Jane smirking, playful and maybe even affectionate.

"Thanks." I chuckle. "I do my best."

"You always do." She sits down next to me.

"You sure you want to get that close?" I'm sure

I stink. Whereas she smells amazing, as always. Like apple blossoms and crisp autumn wind and something uniquely Jane.

"I can handle a little *eau de* football. I'm used to it." She deliberately scoots closer until our thighs touch, and I can feel her warmth like sunshine. Then she lowers her voice so the other players can't hear. "You want to come over and do something on Friday night?"

Does she mean do something or *do something*? Either way, my answer's the same.

"Yeah, for sure. What'd you have in mind?"

"Oh, I don't know. Just hanging out. We can decide when you get there." She fiddles with a loose thread on the hem of her blouse. "Maybe make dinner first?"

"As in, cook together?" That mental picture is so domestic . . . and appealing. "I'd be up for that. Although, I have to warn you. I'm totally useless in the kitchen."

"Don't worry, I am too. We'll figure it out if we put our heads together." She stands up. "Okay, I see Dad coming, which I think means it's time for both of us to get back to work."

I watch her walk away until she disappears inside the training facility.

Coach Royce approaches, and instead of sending us back out on the field, he rests his foot on the bench near me. Without preamble, he asks in an undertone, "Are you sure you know what you're doing, son?"

My heart misses a beat. I have absolutely no fucking idea what I'm doing, but I reply, "It's under control."

Coach studies me, his eyes as hard and sharp as nails, and I resist the urge to drop my gaze. Finally, he says, "I hope so. Because what happened last time . . . I'm not watching her go through that again, so either get out now or stay forever."

He straightens up with a grunt and raises his voice to bark, "Break's over! Get into formation for that new play I showed you at the morning meeting. We're gonna run it until we get it perfect."

I trudge back out onto the field, my stomach and heart and mind still knotted up at Coach's warning, threat, guilt trip, whatever it was.

Just what did he mean by that? Of course I know Jane and I have a history. Of course I don't want to hurt her again. I'm not some stupid asshole . . .

And yet here I am, fucking her anyway.

Someone yells, "What the hell are you doing, Chase?"

I'm right there with ya, buddy.

Then I realize what's actually going on—I let what should have been an easy catch sail right by me and bounce off the turf.

"Sorry!" I call, but I can't bring myself to truly care.

God, what was I thinking? She's my ex and my coach's daughter, and she was almost the teenage mother of my child. Holy shit, what's wrong with me? Now I think we can just be friends with benefits and no one's going to get hurt? Maybe I have been hit in the head too many times.

Everyone grumbles as we get back into position to run the play again. But I'm still too tangled up in my foul, mixed-up temper, and I barely do any better this time . . . or the next time, or the one after that. It's over an hour before Coach finally tells us to hit the showers—more because it's getting dark soon than because we've improved enough to satisfy him, I suspect.

The atmosphere in the locker room is more than a little deflated and grouchy. I've just finished toweling off and getting dressed when Alex taps me on the shoulder.

"Hey, Chase. Mind telling me what the fuck was going on out there?"

I repress a growl. "Yeah, actually, I do mind."

"Was that shit show supposed to be football? I was on the other side of the field, and I could still see y—"

"Dude. I'm seriously not in the mood right now," I grumble.

"What, like you've got more important things to worry about?" Alex pokes me in the chest. "You botched everything today, and it's because you're careless. Are you going to be that careless with *her*?"

My head whips up and I stare at him, my jaw dropped. "What the fuck did you just say?"

"I know something's going on between you and Jane—I'm not blind. The hell is the matter with you?" He shoves his face into mine. "You've already made her cry too many times. Do it again and your ass is done."

My mouth opens and closes a few times, but nothing comes out. Nothing works. Instead, I slam my locker and storm off.

Careless. Not good enough. As pissed off as I am, I can't shake Alex's words, and it makes me want to punch myself instead of him.

Maybe everyone is right. Maybe I'm not up to the task of being with Jane. Dating a professional football player is a hard road to walk. I've seen so many relationships broken up by the game's relentless demands of time, energy, travel, focus . . . not just mine and Trista's, but also those of countless other players and their girlfriends.

Jane already got hurt by that life ten years ago. What kind of man would I be if I dragged her back into it?

I don't want to face it . . . but deep down, I know what I have to do.

CHAPTER *Fifteen*

Jane

When the Hawks' newest quarterback happened to be the longest-standing person on my shit list, I knew I was in for a long parade of the unexpected: unexpected run-ins, unexpected rumors circulating, unexpected crying fits in my office. I could have bet money on all of it.

But never in a million years did I think I would be picturing myself as Weston Chase's girlfriend. It's one thing to expect the unexpected. But falling for Wes isn't just unexpected; it's out of the question. And yet that's exactly what I'm doing.

No, we haven't had the define-the-relationship talk. But based on the last few nights we've spent together, it seems like Wes and I are in the same boat, that boat sailing steadily toward commitment. Nothing about us feels casual, that's for sure.

Besides, if Wes were looking for something casual, there are a hundred and one fangirls drooling over him at every turn who would be happy to crawl into bed with him. Yet I'm the one who has been granted the privilege of waking up to that brilliant smile and sleepy dark blue eyes the past few days. So if he's not interested in anyone else, and I've officially cast him as the only leading man in all of my fantasies, why not call it what it is?

As I sit on my couch, sipping my coffee and watching the morning sun climb in the sky outside my apartment, I picture him here with me. I imagine him frying eggs in the kitchen, his cheeks still flushed from an early morning workout, humming along to a hip-hop song on the radio while I watch him quietly with a cup of coffee. And I know that this is what I want. *He* is what I want.

There's a reason why, after a full decade, I never quite got over Wes, never quite shook the thought of us being together. It was easier to hate him than to address the heartbreak. But now, as we teeter on the edge of being an official couple again, I'm somehow ready to dive in headfirst.

It's insane.

I swallow a big gulp of coffee, the caffeine sending my daydream of playing house with Wes fizzling away, much to my dismay.

But maybe it doesn't have to be a daydream. Maybe we will make it a reality. A romantic night in with an amazing home-cooked meal sounds like just what the doctor ordered. I'm more of a takeout girl since I know about as much about cooking as most girls know about football, but if I could whip up one of Wes's favorite dishes, he'd definitely be impressed. I've got a kitchen full of untouched ingredients and a full day with no plans. Sounds like the perfect recipe for a romantic evening.

I rest my half-empty mug on a coaster and reach for my cell phone, shooting Wes a quick text to ask if he's free tonight before opening up my contacts. I haven't cleared out my phone in ages; I'm almost positive I still have Mrs. Chase's phone number in here somewhere. We always got along back in the day, so hopefully it wouldn't be too out of line for me to give her a call.

There she is, Shirley Chase, listed with both a mobile and a landline. I push my thumb against the mobile number, and it hardly rings once before a bubbly voice picks up the line.

"Well, who would've guessed it, if it isn't little

Miss Jane Royce. Boy, am I glad to hear from you."

Her high-pitched voice is just as sweet as I remember it. She was always so overly enthusiastic, the embodiment of the "Midwest nice" stereotype.

"Hi, Mrs. Chase, it's great to talk to you too. How have you been?"

"Just fine, sweetheart, and I've gotta tell you, I am so proud of you. Big important job as assistant manager to the team."

"Thank you." I chuckle nervously. Her son is the starting quarterback for one of this country's best teams, but she's sweet to compliment my role on the team. "I'm actually calling for a bit of a favor. I'm on a mission to find out Wes's favorite food."

There's an exaggerated gasp on the other end of the line, followed by a satisfied chuckle. "I knew you two were seeing each other again. Well, I just think that's the sweetest."

My mouth spreads into a tight smile in reaction to her use of the phrase "seeing each other." It's so old fashioned. I've done a whole lot more than just see Wes these past few days, but she doesn't need to know that.

Grabbing a pen and an old takeout napkin, I jot down the recipe Mrs. Chase relays to me for Wes's favorite: chicken parmesan. She reminds me multiple times to at least triple the recipe for Wes, muttering that "the boy could eat the whole Christmas ham before you were done saying grace, I swear."

I thank Mrs. Chase profusely for the recipe, which she insists is a simple one. Thank goodness.

We say our good-byes, and when I press the screen to hang up, a text from Wes pops up.

> No plans tonight. You got something in mind? I'd love to see you.

Although I know he doesn't mean anything by it, just reading the word "love" from him makes my heart threaten to thump out of my chest.

Slow down, Jane. It's just a text, not a love letter.

But that doesn't stop my fingers from jittering a bit as my thumbs rush to respond.

> My place at 5? I'm cooking up

something special for us.

I grab my mug and finish the rest of my coffee without taking my eyes off the screen, awaiting his reply. Within moments, I've got a text back.

Sounds perfect. See you then, beautiful.

There's that thumping in my chest again. Something about the big, strong Weston Chase being soft and sweet has always made me feel all gooey inside.

Once I've hooked my phone up to my speaker, I put on my best hip-hop playlist and pile my hair into a messy bun. Step one is getting this apartment date-night ready. Everything is already fairly clean and organized, but tonight, I'm not going for sub-par. I'm going for spectacular.

After vacuuming every square inch of the apartment and dusting every shelf into submission, I venture into the back of my hall closet to see what I have on hand to spruce up our dining experience with a little ambience. There's got to be something in here that's a bit fancier than the current stack of unread mail decorating my kitchen table.

Out of an old cardboard box, I scrounge up a red linen tablecloth and some gold candlesticks from when I hosted Thanksgiving for my parents and me a few years back. Those will work nicely.

I spend all morning making everything just right before running to the grocery store for the few ingredients I'm missing for the chicken parm. While I'm there, I buy a bouquet of white roses to use as the centerpiece, just like the ones from my senior-year prom corsage. I wonder if Wes will remember that they're my favorite. Maybe a few delicate touches of our past won't hurt.

It's a long afternoon of struggling through this recipe, and by the time I slide the chicken parm into the oven, it's already half-past four o'clock. Jeez, if Mrs. Chase said this recipe was simple, I don't want to know what a difficult recipe would look like.

The pile of dishes in my sink makes me want to swear off cooking for good, but imagining the look on Wes's face when he sees I've slaved over his favorite dish is enough to power me through washing every single one.

• • •

Finally, once I have a clean kitchen and dinner

in the oven, I've got very little time to get ready. *Here's to hoping Wes isn't as early tonight as he is for every practice.*

I shower off my day of cooking and cleaning, pick out a slinky maroon dress I've been saving for a special occasion, and curl my honey-blond hair into a waterfall of messy waves. A nude lip and a thick coat of mascara is the perfect *I tried, but not too hard* look.

I check the time on my phone—5:06 and no word from Wes. He's probably looking for parking, which means I have enough time for some finishing touches. And I have just the thing.

Swinging open the door of my medicine cabinet, I dig through the boxes of Band-Aids and old hair products until I find what I'm looking for: the beautiful blue glass bottle of perfume Wes gifted me so many years ago. My former signature scent. I couldn't bear to wear it after we broke up, but it broke my heart too much to think of throwing it away.

Now, as I spritz the sweet, light perfume onto my wrists and neck, I know why I held on to it. After ten years of burying it in the back of my medicine cabinet, I know when Wes presses his lips against my neck tonight, he'll breathe me in and remember how in love we used to be, how in love we could be again.

Another time check—5:10. It's unlike Wes to be running behind, but I don't want to be too clingy and text him over a ten-minute delay. Instead, I opt for the liquor cabinet, dressing up two tall glasses with limes for gin and tonics. I promise to nurse mine, swearing I won't finish it before Wes gets here. I grab a seat on the couch and take a slow, measured sip from my glass, setting Wes's out for him on the coffee table.

I think about that night in his apartment when he reached to swap his full drink with my empty one, his arm intentionally grazing my thigh and making every hair on my body stand on end. God, whatever this man does to me, he does it well, and I can't wait for him to arrive.

When my slow, measured sips bring me to the bottom of my glass, I do another time check. It's almost six o'clock, and still no word from Wes. Did he lie down for a nap and forget to set an alarm or something?

Dinner is already done, waiting for us on the stovetop. It's going to get cold if he doesn't arrive soon, and my hard work won't taste nearly as good reheated. Annoyed, I snatch up my phone and call him, but after two rings, it goes to voice mail. I hang up and try again, but I'm met with the same results. Really?

Another half hour crawls by as I stare at the wall, finishing off the second gin and tonic. Nothing. Not a word. I call him twice more. Radio silence.

Fuck this.

I stomp into the kitchen, eyeing the now cold chicken parm. All that hard work for what, to be stood up? What a load of shit. I turn on the faucet and flip on the garbage disposal, which gargles and snarls to life as I dump my hours of effort down the drain.

Good-bye, chicken parm. Good-bye, romantic evening. Hello, night of crying on the couch.

I reach for my phone and press Alex's name just as my throat tightens and the tears start to roll. He picks up on the first ring.

"What's up, Jane? I'm surprised you're not with Wes."

Wrong thing to say, Alex. A pitiful sob escapes from the back of my throat.

"Shit, okay," he says quickly. "Are you at

home? I can be there in ten. Do you need me?"

I muster up a *yes* to both questions, and before I have a chance to decide what romance movie I'm going to cry over tonight, I hear his voice in my foyer. I can always count on Alex to let himself right in.

"All right, do I have to kick some quarterback ass or what?"

I wipe the tears from my cheeks with the back of my hand. "No. Sort of. Maybe just a little." I sniff. "He stood me up, Alex. He didn't call or text or anything."

"Shit, Jane. I'm so sorry." Alex takes the spot next to me on the couch. "The place looks great. He's missing out. What were your plans?"

"I made this big fancy dinner. And then I just had to . . ." I trail off, gesturing at the sink that served as the chicken parm's burial site. "What a waste. Of food, of a day. A total waste."

"You dumped it?" Alex's eyes widen. "Dude, we totally could've polished that off together. You want to order Thai food or something? My treat."

When I nod, he picks out a place that delivers and orders half the menu.

As soon as it arrives, we scoop up heaping helpings of noodles and rice onto paper plates, and my phone buzzes on the coffee table. We both know without even looking at the screen that it has to be Wes.

"You sure you want to read that?" Alex asks, chopsticks in midair. "I can just delete it if you want."

"No, I want to read it."

I set my plate down and grab my phone, take a deep breath, and open the text, hoping for the excuse of a lifetime. Instead, I get this:

`I'm not the guy you need. I'm sorry. You had it right all those years ago. Good-bye, Jane.`

I read it once, then twice, then ten or twenty times over. Is this some sort of joke? I stare at my phone, waiting for some kind of a follow-up text, a "just kidding." Maybe another teammate stole his phone again like last time. But nothing comes.

"You okay?" Alex asks hesitantly.

I shake my head and slam my phone facedown. The Thai food looks delicious, but I feel like I could throw up. Just like he did all those years ago, Wes has left me high and dry.

"Let's just forget it," I say, shaking my head. My stomach tosses and turns as I grab one long noodle with my chopsticks and hold it up in front of me, assessing whether or not I can choke food down.

I remember at Wes's apartment the other night when he literally swept me off my feet. Thinking about the way he looked at me that night brings back the familiar pressure of tears building that stings the top of my cheeks. He looked at me like that all those years ago too. Why did I think this time around would be any different?

Alex lets out a frustrated sigh. "He's an idiot, Jane. A huge fucking idiot."

And I know he's right. But it doesn't make it hurt any less.

After I get another round of tears out, Alex insists that I at least try to eat.

"Don't let him win," he says, slugging me in the arm. "Don't let him ruin Thai food. Thai food is sacred."

That gets a snicker out of me.

"Made you laugh. Now you have to eat!" Alex says, a victorious smile spreading across his face.

I roll my eyes, picking up my chopsticks again. The only things I've put into my stomach today are black coffee and gin and tonics. I guess I can manage a little food.

It takes almost the full night of us watching game-show reruns on the couch, but I manage to clear my plate. I don't even mind the curry stains I get on my slinky maroon dress. I'm just happy not to be alone, to have a best friend like Alex who's willing to show up at the drop of a hat and make things better.

Halfway through our fourth episode of *Jeopardy*, I nod off, and Alex nudges me awake.

"C'mon, sleepyhead." He laughs, helping me off the couch. "Let's get you to bed. I've got to hit the road."

He walks me to my bedroom, turning away so I can change into pajamas. He's part best friend, part babysitter, leaning against the wall as I brush my teeth. When I'm done, he pulls back the blankets so I can crawl into bed.

"Hey, Jane?" Alex says, his fingers hovering over the light switch. "Don't text him tonight, okay? Promise?"

I nod my head. That's a promise I know I can keep.

CHAPTER *Sixteen*

Weston

"You get enough to eat, honey?" Mom asks over our thick slices of apple pie.

"God, yes. I'm about to explode." I lean back with a defeated groan, my chair creaking. "You really pulled out all the stops, Mom. I won't be hungry for the rest of the weekend."

Pot roast, glazed carrots, scalloped potatoes, and now dessert . . . I'm so full it almost hurts, but I'm not complaining. Although I am still wondering something.

"So, not that I don't love seeing you, but was there some reason you were in such a hurry about meeting up?" She'd been calling at least once a day for the past week, asking when was the soonest I could come over for lunch.

“Can’t a mother want to steal a little time with her only child?”

I sigh, but there’s much more affection in it than exasperation. “Of course you can. And I’ve been looking forward to catching up too. It’s been too long.”

“I’m so happy you’re back home. For selfish reasons, of course, but I also know things didn’t go well for you in Philadelphia.” She uses her fork to push a bite of pie around on her plate. “By the way,” she says too innocently, “whatever happened to that Jane girl? She was so sweet.”

My overstuffed stomach twinges, and I give my mom a confused look. “You know what happened, Mom. She dumped me.”

“No, I don’t mean when you were in college,” she singsongs, her eyes sparkling.

“Then what are y—” I almost slam my fork down. “For God’s sake, Mom, not you too.” Did someone take out a billboard or something? Does everybody and their kid brother have an opinion on our relationship? “How’d you even find out about any of this?”

Mom can’t keep her grin contained anymore. “Jane called me last Friday to get my secret chicken parm recipe."

Shit. It takes me only a second to realize this was for the dinner I didn't show up to. When I dumped Jane over a goddamn text message because I'm an idiot and a coward, and I knew my resolve would crumple if I saw her in person.

My gut clenches all the way up to my throat. "And she told you we were . . ." *Dating? Fucking? Making a huge mistake that would only hurt her in the end?* "Involved?" That would certainly explain why Mom was so urgent about having lunch together ASAP.

"She didn't have to. Calling up your mom out of the blue, asking how to cook what just so happens to be your favorite dinner?" She gives me a sly look and taps her temple. "This old lady can figure a few things out."

I can't decide whether to be relieved that Jane didn't reveal anything, or frustrated at the lost chance to find out more about what she thinks of me. Then I remember that's none of my business anymore. We're over . . . not that we ever really began again in the first place. And it's for the best.

"So?" Mom coos. I swear she even wiggles a little. "Tell me more! How long have you been dating? Is it official yet?"

"We broke up."

The words are like glass shards forced up my throat. I stare at my plate so I don't have to see Mom's face fall, but I can still hear her disappointment in her voice, and it makes me too aware of how raw I feel.

"Oh, honey . . . I'm so sorry. I didn't know, or I wouldn't have brought it up."

"I know. It's fine." My voice is flat, tight with the effort to hold back how sick and spun up I feel.

She reaches across the table to stroke my clenched hand. "You must feel terr—"

"I don't want to talk about it."

There's nothing *to* talk about. It's a done deal. I just have to stay strong and give Jane space. Just have to keep reminding myself that this is for the best.

I must have done the right thing. Because if I didn't . . .

I can't let how much I miss Jane tempt me into finishing that thought.

I force myself to pick up my fork and dig back

into the pie. Mom's cooking is delicious as always, but right now, eating feels more like shoveling sand into a hole than a pleasant visit to childhood memories.

For a while, we mechanically chew, swallow, and repeat while painful silence fills the space around us. Then Mom mutters, "What's that noise?"

I prick up my ears and hear a faint buzz from the mudroom. I left my phone in my coat pocket so I wouldn't be tempted to check it during my time hanging out with my mom. Normally, I'd ignore it until I left, but the way it repeats sounds like a call rather than a text, and I can't think who'd be calling me other than work.

I grunt and stand up. "Be right back."

My phone shows nine missed calls and six voice mails from a number I don't recognize. *What the hell?*

I play the first voice mail and am greeted by Alex yelling, "Wes, pick up your fucking phone!" at the top of his lungs.

How did Alex even get my number? But his next words drive every other thought out of my head.

"Coach had a heart attack! The ambulance just took him to Riverview General, and if you don't go help her, I swear to God, I'll—"

I click my phone off and jam it back in my pocket. "Sorry, Mom, I've got to run."

"What's wrong?" She stands up from the dining room table, looking alarmed.

"Jane's dad is in the hospital. I'll call you later when I know more." I yank on my coat, my heart pounding so fast, my hands shake and the zipper gets stuck.

Fuck it. I don't have time for this. I'll fix it later. I can handle a little cold wind in the meantime.

"Oh dear, not Ken. That poor man, he was always so good to you. Here, let me pack up the rest of the pie for you."

"You don't have to—" I stop quickly to peck her cheek. "Thanks, Mom."

She presses one hand to my cheek. "Of course. Now, go be with her."

I'm already in the car and flooring the gas before I realize that I'm supposed to be giving Jane space right now. But none of that matters at the moment.

CHAPTER Seventeen

Jane

"There has to be some sort of mistake."

I'm clutching my cell phone with one hand and the edge of my desk with the other, trying to keep from falling over. I refuse to believe this is happening.

The nurse on the phone is calm and collected, but I'm frantic, praying that she's got it all wrong, that my father is completely healthy. But she insists on repeating the truth I don't want to hear. Ken Royce, my father, has had a heart attack and is in the hospital. And from the tone of the nurse's voice, things must not be looking good.

The walls of my office shift and spin around me as I feel my head go light as air and I let myself fall back into my desk chair.

This is the kind of thing that happens to other people, not to my family. I'm the one who writes the get-well-soon cards, and worse yet, the sympathy cards. I'm not the one who receives them.

Dad is healthy, active, always running around the field and eating a good diet. Just the other day at dinner, he loaded up on second helpings of salad. He's never given the doctors anything to worry about before. Sure, he's not exactly young and spry anymore, but his health has always been leaps and bounds better than most men his age. Well, up until now.

The nurse apologizes in a low, somber voice, then gives me information about the hospital, the room he's in, and what happens next. I scramble to find a sticky note and jot everything down, but my handwriting is hardly legible.

Can't I stop shaking long enough to write down the goddamn information?

She informs me that Dad won't be available for visitation for a little while, that he'll be going through some additional tests. She lists them off, explaining to me what the next steps are, but the medical terms goes in one ear and out the other. I can hardly focus on breathing; I don't stand a chance of retaining a bunch of medical lingo.

Right now, I don't want her to tell me the difference between a chest X-ray and an MRI. I want her to tell me my dad is going to be okay. But neither of us knows if that's true.

I thank the nurse, although I'm honestly not sure what for, and hang up the phone, expecting to burst into tears the second I hit END CALL. But I don't. Not right away, at least. I'm trembling, my gut wrenching as I stare at the address I've written down on the sticky note. But I'm paralyzed. I can feel tears building behind my nose and cheeks, but they won't spill out.

• • •

When I arrive at the hospital, my mom looks positively wrecked. Her eyes are red and swollen, and I immediately burst into tears when I see her. We stand in the waiting room, hugging for an eternity, until finally I take a deep breath and pull back to meet her eyes.

"Is he going to be okay?" My voice is shaky and soft.

Mom sniffs and tucks her hair behind her ears. "They're running some tests. I don't know if we'll get to see him tonight."

She didn't answer my question, but maybe that's better. I don't know if I'm strong enough to handle the truth right now.

My stomach is in knots as Mom and I sit down in the vinyl chairs. Silence stretches between us as I hold her hand. And then Wes barges into my hospital waiting room, and every barrier I have comes tumbling down.

"Jane, are you okay?" His voice is exasperated, his eyes panicked. I guess word spreads fast when the head coach is in trouble.

Despite everything Wes has done to me, when he spreads his arms open, I spring out of my chair and run right into them, the tears finally pouring out. For now, I'll forget that he stood me up, forget that horrible text he sent and how much I've been hurting the past few days. None of that is half as important as my dad.

I bury my face into Wes's chest, and he holds me firmly against him.

"It's okay. It's all going to be okay," he murmurs, cradling the back of my head as I sob into his shirt. "Your dad is going to be fine."

I feel so safe here in Wes's arms, that for a split second, I believe him. But then I remember the worry in the nurse's voice, and my throat tightens again.

"We could lose him, Wes," I manage to say between sobs, clutching at the dampened fabric of his T-shirt. "We could lose him, and I didn't even get to say good-bye."

"Your dad? Hell no." There's genuine surprise in Wes's voice as he pulls me just far enough away from him to look me in the eye, wiping the tears off my cheek with his thumb. "Your dad is the toughest son of a bitch I know. He can fight through anything. You must've gotten that from him."

The corner of my mouth curls into the tiniest smile as I slowly catch my breath, the tears slowing down. He's right. Dad is tough as hell, and so am I. Neither of us is giving up yet.

"I'm just so scared, Wes," I say, wiping the tears with the back of my hand. God, I can't believe how much I've cried in front of him these past few weeks. It's probably more than he saw me cry the whole time we were together.

Wes folds me gently back into his arms. "It's all right, Jane. We're all a little scared." And by the slight shakiness in his voice, I can tell he's not excluding himself. He smooths my hair with his hand and doesn't let go until I've released the last sob I can muster, my frame falling limp in his arms.

Two hours ago, if Weston Chase would have so much as stepped foot in my presence, I would have called him an asshole and told him to delete my number. But right now, contrary to every ounce of logic within me, there's no one I'd rather be with.

He guides us to the chair beside my mom, and he gives her a quick hug too, whispering how sorry he is.

Mom gives him a sad smile.

"Sorry about your shirt," I mumble once the tears subside.

He looks down at his tear- and snot-soaked T-shirt and shrugs. "I don't think that's really what's important right now."

He's looking at me, but I don't want to look him in the eye right now. I might start crying again for different reasons. I'm glad he's here, but we can't just pretend things are fine between us.

For almost a full minute, we remain like this: him looking at me, and me looking anywhere except directly at him. I can't. It hurts too much.

Weston leaves to get my mom a cup of coffee,

and when he comes back, he's also carrying a couple of water bottles. I eagerly take one and drink. I have no idea what time it is, or even what day, my brain is so clouded by everything.

"Are you planning on staying here tonight, Mrs. Royce?" Wes asks my mom.

She blows on her coffee and takes a sip. "Yeah. I wouldn't know what to do with myself in that big, empty house."

"I'll stay with you," I offer.

Mom reaches for my hand and shakes her head. "Your father will be busy with tests tonight, and I'm sure we won't get any answers until tomorrow. Why don't you come back in the morning?"

I don't argue with my mom. Part of me wants to stay here with her, and the other part of me wants to go lie in my bed and cry myself to sleep.

"I can swing by your place and pick you up an overnight bag," Wes says.

Mom nods. "Thank you, Weston."

"Do you want me to take you home?" Wes asks, now looking at me. "It's probably not safe for you to drive right now. I want to be sure you make it home okay."

"A ride home would be great, yes," I say, glancing up at him, and Wes looks relieved that I actually accepted his offer.

Yes, I'd rather get home without his help, but I also know I shouldn't be on the road if I could burst into tears again at any second. I have to hope this will all turn out okay. It's all I have right now—hope that Dad is strong enough to fight through this horrible nightmare.

I give my mom a squeeze, and make her promise to call if there's news. Then I follow Wes out to the parking lot, and he opens the passenger door of his rental car for me. I wonder if he'll ever get around to actually buying a car of his own. As we drive through the outskirts of Chicago, I try to focus on the skyline, the planes flying overhead, anything that will keep away the thought of Dad lying alone in a cold, sterile hospital bed.

Wes turns on my favorite hip-hop station, but for once, I don't feel like singing along. I don't even feel like talking. I just keep my eyes locked on the road ahead. I've got to keep moving forward. That's all we can do.

When we get to my street, Wes zooms past it, and I shoot him a confused look.

"Food. You should eat," he says bluntly.

He pulls the car into a drive-through and places my usual order for a cheeseburger and onion rings without asking. His memory is like a steel trap. He pays for the food, and the girl in the drive-through hands over the greasy paper bag.

"Comfort food," he says with a grin as he passes it off to me.

My stomach is still uneasy with worry, but I munch on a few onion rings on the quick drive back.

We pull up to my apartment building, and I'm surprised when Wes shifts the car into park and turns off the engine. I was expecting him to just drop me off and go.

"Is it okay if I walk you in?"

First the drive-through, now this? Is this his definition of an apology? Part of me wants to give him shit for it, but I'm too exhausted to bicker. I just want to eat and go to bed.

"Yeah, that's fine."

I unclick my seat belt and hop out of the car, Wes trailing closely behind me. Once we're inside, I kick off my shoes and plop down on the couch with my legs crossed, my bag of comfort food nestled in my lap.

"Can I grab you a plate?" he asks, and I shake my head, reaching into the bag for another onion ring.

Should I ask him to leave? Should I ask him to sit down? My head is too much of a war zone right now to know what I want. Other than this burger. I know for sure that I want this burger.

"You can sit," I finally say politely.

It feels weird to have him standing there in the kitchen, but I know if he leaves, I'll be alone with the thousand and one worst-case scenarios running through my brain. I flip on the TV to the game-show channel to keep the awkward silence away as I work through my bag of fried food.

It's barely eight, but I'm fading fast. The sooner I get to sleep, the sooner tomorrow comes, and maybe tomorrow the nurse will call back. Maybe tomorrow, I'll get to see Dad.

"Bedtime?" Wes asks. He must have spied my heavy eyelids.

"I think that would be best," I say, crumpling up the empty fast-food bag and tossing it into the trash across the room. "I think I'm just going to stay on the couch. Fall asleep watching TV."

I turn the volume down on the remote and curl up on the couch, cueing Wes that it's time to go. He grabs the blanket off the back of the armchair and heads toward me, draping it carefully over me. I give him an expectant look like he might kiss me good night, but he just tucks in the edges of the blanket and turns away.

"I'm going to get your mom an overnight bag, garage code still the same?" he asks.

How in the world does he remember that? I nod.

"Call me if you need anything," he says as he heads for the door.

I can barely keep my eyes open, but just before I fall asleep, I hear the door click open and closed again.

Goddamn. Wes can be really sweet when he's not being a complete asshole.

CHAPTER Eighteen

Weston

A nurse pokes her head into the waiting room. "Jane? Weston?" We both leap to our feet, and she holds up her hand with an apologetic smile. "Ken wants to talk to both of you, but I'll have to take you in one at a time. He still can't handle too much excitement."

Before Jane can say anything, I tell her, "Go on."

She hurries to join the nurse and be escorted back to her father's hospital room. I take the opportunity to grab a cup of coffee and stretch out the stiffness from waiting on that tiny, hard plastic chair.

The nurse returns about half an hour later to

lead me down the mazelike hallways. She doesn't need to bother—I've been here almost every day for the past week, so I know the route by heart—but I appreciate her quiet, efficiently professional company.

When we arrive, I'm both disappointed and relieved to find only Coach Royce and his wife, Nancy, in the room. Jane's mom must have finally put her foot down and sent Jane home.

She desperately needs the rest; she's barely left the hospital since the ambulance brought her dad in. And although I hate to admit it, spending so much time with Jane has racked my nerves as well as soothed them. Everything has become agonizingly awkward, and I never know how to act around her anymore.

"How are you?" I ask Coach. He looks haggard still, but undeniably better than yesterday. It's hard to believe his surgery was only a week ago.

"I'm feeling all right," he replies, his voice only a little gravelly. "And the doctors say my prognosis looks great. One more night of observation, and they'll release me tomorrow morning."

This is fantastic news. Everyone on the team will be so relieved to hear it.

So, why do I still feel wrung out inside?

Coach says, "I'll be back in the saddle in two weeks. In the meantime—"

"No, dear, they said six," Nancy says, interrupting to remind him. "Work is too stressful."

He grunts dismissively. "He said I shouldn't go out on the *field* for six weeks. If I can't oversee practice drills, I need to at least attend team meetings, for crying out loud."

When Nancy shoots him a *we'll talk about this later* frown, Coach turns his attention back to me. "Anyway, you boys listen to the assistant coach. Don't slack off just 'cause I'm gone, ya hear?"

I force a chuckle, thinking of how abysmally I've been playing ever since I stopped seeing Jane. "Wouldn't dream of it, Coach."

He studies me, his eyes narrowing in suspicion. "You been eating all right, son? Getting enough sleep?"

Not even close. "Yes, sir."

He still looks skeptical. "Well, you look about as bad as I feel. Whatever the problem is, figure it out and deal with it before our next game."

I nod, knowing that I can't.

• • •

I sigh in disgust as I open my locker. Today's practice was yet another embarrassing shit show. I can't concentrate, and there's no strength in my throws or sprints, no finesse in my footwork.

I rub my eyes. I'm fucking exhausted. Every night, I lie in bed for hours before sleep finally decides to grace me with its presence. Maybe tonight will be different . . . but I doubt it.

Pull it together, Chase. Just focus on one thing at a time. Take off uniform, shower, put on clothes, decide what the hell I'm going to do for dinner when I have no appetite and everything tastes like sand.

On my way out of the locker room, a hand lands on my shoulder, and I turn to see Alex.

"Can we talk for a minute?" he says.

I sigh, and my response comes out dull and listless. "What do you want?" I can't even muster the energy to snap at him.

"I meant in private."

I give him a wary look, trying to determine if

he really just wants to talk, or if this little chat will end in a fight. But his face is solemn, with no trace of his usual taste for sparring.

Finally, I say, "Okay, fine, I'll bite. Just stop looking like someone died. You're freaking me out."

"Deal." He pushes the locker room door open.

I follow him to a deserted corner of the hall. "So, what's this all about? You just trying to get me alone to kick my ass or something?"

Alex presses his lips into a tight line and exhales loudly through his nose. "You're already doing a great job of kicking your own ass. No, I wanted to say . . . I'm sorry."

I stare at him. "You're sorry? About what?"

"What the hell do you think, man? You and Jane!"

My confusion morphs into shock.

"I know you thought this was for the best," he says, "but it's not. You've been moping around for weeks, and you're playing so bad, you're ruining practice for everybody else." He gives me a measuring look. "And she'd kill me if she knew I told you this, but Jane is miserable too."

"She misses me? Still?"

My spirits lift for a second before guilt crushes them again. Only an asshole would feel happy that she's sad. This only confirms she's better off without me. And then there was what everybody else said about us . . .

"But you and Coach told me to leave her alone."

"I was wrong, okay? I shouldn't have pushed you into breaking up with her. Don't make me say it again." Alex pauses. "Wait, Coach asked you to dump his daughter?"

I shrug. "Not exactly. He said I should either leave now or stay forever."

"So, let me get this straight. Jane's father, your boss, the man with every reason to shut this down with extreme prejudice, instead told you to shit or get off the pot. And you chose the latter?" He shakes his head with a slight smile. "You really are an idiot, you know that?"

Clearly not. "Okay, fuck off," I mutter. "It doesn't matter anymore anyway. Whatever we had is dead now. I killed it."

Alex rolls his eyes. "So you screwed up. Big deal, we all fumble sometimes. What matters is how you fix your mistakes. Get off your ass and go win back your girl."

I don't know whether to laugh or to scowl. "As fun as it would be to prove you wrong, I don't think that's likely."

"You aren't even going to try? You'll just roll over and let me have her?" Alex smirks, all dimples and swagger.

My jaw drops. "*You*?"

"Sure, she's heartbroken now, but she'll get over you eventually. And when she does, I'll be right there, waiting in the wings. The perfect rebound. I'll love her up, marry her, put my baby inside her . . ."

"The hell you will!" I snarl.

I know damn well he's just trying to piss me off, and it's totally fucking working. At the mental image his words conjures, Jane full and round with someone else's baby, I'm ready to snap from all the primal, possessive rage building up inside me.

His shit-eating grin tells me Alex knows he's scored a point. "What, you going to do something to stop me?" He shrugs his shoulders arrogantly. "Weren't you just saying you'd given up?"

I glower at him. "I never said that."

"Could've fooled me. It definitely sounded like you were done with Jane, and you didn't care what happened to her anymore."

"Of course I care about her! I'd do anything for her. That's why I let her go."

"What a bunch of bullshit. You didn't let her go—you wussed out and ran away. You were scared of a future you couldn't control, of all the ass-busting work it takes to be a good partner." Alex's eyes flash, his nostrils flaring. "And you broke her heart *again*."

My teeth are clenched so tightly, my jaw aches. But no matter how hard I search, I can't find any comebacks. Can't deny his accusation that I acted like a coward. And if cutting Jane off really did make her suffer . . .

Fuck.

I'm an idiot.

"If you'd really 'do anything' for Jane, then you should've pulled your shit together and buckled down. You should've put her feelings first, not decided what was best for her without even telling her what the fuck was going on in that empty head of yours. So I'm gonna ask you one last time. Are you really going to let her go forever, without even putting up a fight?"

We stare each other down for a long minute. But in the end, there's only one thing to say.

"You wish, asshole!"

"There's the Weston Chase I know and tolerate." Alex punches me lightly in the shoulder. "Now, go get your ass in gear, you stupid fuck."

"Thanks . . . and fuck you." I stomp off, already cooking up a plan.

CHAPTER Nineteen

Jane

"You must be Jane."

The brown-haired, blue-eyed man standing in the entrance of the sushi restaurant must be the guy I'm waiting for. He looks exactly like the picture my mom showed me on her phone, which is more than I can say about most of the blind dates I've been on.

"Kevin?" I tilt my head coyly, trying to conceal the shock in my voice.

It's not like I was expecting the guy to be a total troll, it's just that I don't have the world's best track record when it comes to blind dates. At this point in my life, I can safely assume any guy I'm being set up with is going to be a total clunker, emotionally unavailable, or just trying to score free Hawks tickets, the last of which I can't really blame him for. Kevin might still be a flop, but at least he's handsome, so that's a strong start.

"Yes. Nice to meet you," he says warmly, smiling at me.

When my mom mentioned setting me up with the son of her friend from book club, I knew she was just grasping at opportunities to get me out of her hair and out of my own head. I know I've been driving her up the wall.

Since work gave me all the time off I need after Dad's heart attack, I spend most of the day hovering around the house and spewing worst-case scenarios about Dad's health, despite him recovering just fine. Better than fine, really. The nurse at his last appointment said he was on track for a full recovery in record time, but that hasn't stopped me from gnawing at my cuticles and grilling Mom with questions about his medical history and cholesterol levels.

So I agreed to let this guy buy me sushi to give my mom a little room to breathe. If I'm lucky, maybe this date will even get my mind off a certain quarterback for an evening. Killing two birds with one chopstick. At least, a girl can hope.

Kevin pulls me in for an informal but slightly awkward hug. I can't help but notice how skinny he seems, but then again, any guy is going to seem skinny after you've cozied up to a pro football player. As the hostess leads us to our table, I promise myself that will be my first and last thought about Wes for the evening.

As we take our seats and open our menus, Kevin hits me with the same opening line I've heard a dozen times. "So, I hear you work for the Hawks."

A proud smile spreads across my face. "I sure do. Best team in the league. What about you? What do you do?"

He starts in on a long-winded explanation about his career in software sales, pausing only to order us a bottle of cabernet—after clearing with me that I drink reds, of course. Cute guy, normal job, hasn't brought up a crazy ex-girlfriend or living in his mother's basement yet. Maybe I've served my time on enough crappy blind dates, and it's finally my turn for a good one.

"But enough about me," he says, reaching for his glass of wine. "You work in professional football. That must be a trip."

"Actually, with all the away games, I would

say it's a lot of trips," I say with a smirk, but Kevin doesn't even crack a grin. I can't help but think that Wes would have laughed at that joke.

"Do you like it?" Kevin asks, squinting at me suspiciously.

"Like it?" I laugh. "It's my whole life. I grew up going to Hawks games with my dad all the time. He's the head coach now, so I guess football is just in our DNA. The whole game is such a rush from start to finish, and these guys are so crazy driven." My mind immediately turns to one player in particular, so I add, "Every single one of them."

Kevin crinkles his nose in distaste. Maybe the wine is bad?

I take a sip. Nope, it's just fine.

"So you work directly with the *players*?" Kevin says, dragging out the word *players* as if he were saying *dirty socks* or *moldy cheese*.

"Well, yeah. I'm the assistant manager. That's kind of a huge part of my job."

He shrugs, swirling the wine in his glass. "I'm not really a football fan. I don't watch or anything. But those guys just seem so . . . I don't know. They're like Neanderthals or something. How does a girl like you work with them all the time?"

The waitress appears as I jolt up in my seat, saving me from snapping back at that Neanderthals comment. And what does he mean by "a girl like me"? He's known me for all of five minutes.

Kevin orders a few rolls, but I tell the waitress I'll just stick to wine, suddenly not feeling particularly hungry. He scrunches his eyebrows at me in confusion, but I force a tight smile and close my menu. Looks like this blind date is another clunker after all.

Sure, this guy is moderately handsome, and I'm sure he'd be perfect for a lot of girls. But not me. I could never fall for someone like him, someone who doesn't understand such a crucial aspect of my life. I'm not necessarily looking for a guy who knows who won every Super Bowl. He doesn't have to be football obsessed. But he does have to be a football fan, a football appreciator, or maybe—

A lump forms in my throat, and I swallow it as I complete the thought that I wish I wasn't having.

Or maybe a football player.

Maybe Wes was right from the beginning when he said that I always did have a thing for football players. Or maybe, more specifically, I've just always had a thing for him.

He was so sweet while Dad was in the hospital, always ready to help out any way that he could. He broke things off with me, he has no obligation to my family, and yet he was still there when I needed him the most. Maybe there's a reason he came back into my life. Maybe it's no accident that I can't seem to shake him.

"Hello? Jane?"

With a shudder and a few blinks, I return to reality. A dismal reality where I'm sitting across the table from a guy I have no interest in. And all I want is to escape back into my daydream.

Instead, I take another long sip of my wine.

Weston

My heart rate spikes when I hear Jane's muffled, but unmistakable voice. I shouldn't be surprised she came to work even earlier than I did. With her dad's heart condition and our breakup, it's understandable that she's thrown herself into work. Hell, I've been doing the exact same thing.

As I push open the door to the inner hall, I see she's chatting with the janitor, her slim back to me.

"Howdy," he says when he sees me. "You're here early."

Jane's shoulders twitch. She turns to face me with an expression of careful, fragile neutrality. "Good morning."

That hyper-professional mask is familiar, but this time, it's not hiding anger. The hurt buried deep in her eyes makes my chest ache.

I'll make it right, I vow, making her a silent promise. I worked on my plan for hours last night, and as soon as we get the chance to talk, I have something that I hope will heal everything.

In the meantime, I can't just stare blankly at them. What was this guy's name again? Fred? No, Frank. I've never talked to him much, but he seems like a nice old man.

"Yeah, I woke up at four thirty and couldn't fall back asleep. Figured I might as well get started on strength training."

Frank nods with a *hmm* of understanding. Nobody speaks. They're clearly not going to continue with their conversation while I'm here.

Well, I'm more than happy to puncture this awkward atmosphere. "See you later," I say, and start off to the locker room.

But when I'm about halfway down the hall, Frank says to Jane, "A little bird told me you had a date last night."

I freeze for an instant, then hurry around the

corner, trying to act like I didn't hear anything.

A date? Jane's already started dating again? My stomach clenches almost violently at that knowledge. Fuck, am I too late?

Fear makes the hair on the back of my neck stand up. It's entirely possible that I messed around too long and made too many mistakes, and now I want to ram my head through this cinderblock wall because I might have blown my chance.

I shouldn't eavesdrop. I really shouldn't. But I'm too desperate for more information to force myself to move.

"Seriously?" Jane groans. "Is my father the one feeding you this information?"

Frank wisely doesn't explain how he found out. "So? How'd it go?" His voice has the prodding tone of a doting father.

"It wasn't a big deal." I know she's shrugging without looking at her. Probably knotting her fingers together too.

Evidently, Frank is also wondering what the fuck that means, because he asks, "Was there something wrong with him?"

If he hurt her, I'll hunt him down and rip his

balls off.

Jane makes a noncommittal noise. "We just didn't click."

Thank God. I almost slump back against the wall.

"That's too bad," Frank says. "Well, there's always the next one."

My relief drains away as quickly as it came. Frank is right . . . sure, this guy was a dud, but if she's actively searching, it's only a matter of time until she finds someone who isn't. It probably won't even take very long. After all, she's perfect. Any man would be lucky to have her. She can have her pick of the litter.

Rage washes over me. Why did I act like such a fucking idiot? What was I thinking? How did I screw this up so badly?

My hands shake as I change into my workout clothes. I storm into the weight room and work the chest-press machine like I'm trying to punish myself, barely noticing the 450-pound load, too furious at my own dumbassery and too haunted by mental images of Jane with another man.

I've calmed down only slightly by the time my

teammates start trickling in.

Colin stops by me and comments, “Dude, you’re crushing it today.”

“What? Oh. Thanks.” I go back to murdering the leg-curl machine.

He doesn’t leave. Eventually he asks, “Are you okay, Chase?”

This time I stop to look back at him. The pause makes me finally register how bad my hamstrings burn. “Yeah, man, I’m just thinking.”

“Okay . . .” He sounds skeptical, but lets it go and continues on his way to the weight rack.

Really, there’s nothing to think about anymore. I know damn well what I have to do. Stop pussy-footing around. No more fear and self-doubt. No more hesitating and waiting for the right moment. I’ve run out of time for that shit. I have to make my move *now* . . . and I have an idea on how to go about it.

I rush through the rest of my workout routine and shower so I can be the first to arrive at the team meeting. Jane is already there, along with Coach Royce, sitting in a wheelchair at the front of the room. She looks away as soon as she spots me, but

Coach raises his hand in a cursory wave.

I walk to him and lean down to speak quietly. "Can I make a short presentation? It'll take ten minutes, tops. I promise."

His eyebrows knit. "I suppose so. What's this all about, son?"

"It'll speak for itself." *I hope so, anyway.* "But I'll have to borrow your laptop. I'm kinda flying by the seat of my pants here." I find the file on my phone and send it.

He checks his email, and his eyebrows wing up at the attachment's name. Then he smiles. "I think I have some idea where this is going, but I'll let you handle it your own way."

I nod gratefully and get to work fiddling with cables. I convince Coach's computer to cooperate with the overhead projector just as everyone else finishes finding their seats.

All right, Operation Hijack Team Meeting is a go.

"Excuse me, everyone," I say. "I've got something I gotta say." I cue up my presentation's title slide:

DEAR JANE

Several people mutter to each other. Someone in the back of the room stifles a snicker. But the only reaction I care about is Jane's . . . and she's staring at me in bewilderment.

I quash my sudden urge to chicken out. Come on, man, you haven't even started yet. Push through.

I click to the first slide. It's titled EXHIBIT A and shows a grainy photo of us from our high school yearbook. She's draped in my too-big football jersey, and I have my arm around her shoulders, wearing a dazed, smitten grin like I can't believe my own luck.

"You were the first girl I ever loved."

Jane's eyes widen and her lips part in shock. There's a few more whispers, but the room is surprisingly quiet. Everyone's watching Jane and me in curiosity.

"And who could blame me for falling?"

The next slide is a newspaper photo of a Hawks press conference where Jane stands onstage with Mr. Flores, her expression as keen as her outfit, not a hair out of place. She looks hot as shit.

"You're smart, dedicated, hardworking to a fault, a total football junkie . . ." A photo of her favorite rapper flashes on the screen. "Plus, it's so much fun to hear you belting out gangster rap in your office when you think nobody's around."

There's a ripple of scattered chuckles. It may be my imagination, but Jane's eyes seem to glisten.

"Not only that, but we make a kickass team."

Exhibit C is a stock image of orange and black socks. That gets blank stares from everybody except Jane and the cornerback Ramirez, who laughs at the memory of Philadelphia.

"Seriously, though . . . when we put our heads together, I feel like I can handle any problem."

Next comes a low-res snapshot of her with her Dad, their arms slung over each other's shoulders. She's constantly giving up her free time to devote herself to helping her parents, both on and off the football field.

"And you're kind too."

Jane smiles up at the screen, even as she blinks back tears.

Exhibit E is just a bulleted list, but I'm glad now that I couldn't find a decent photo last night, because my stomach's wound itself so tightly, I'd never remember what I was planning to say without notes.

"Just the sight of you has the power to make me smile. Even if I'm having the world's crappiest day, as soon as you're there, it's like I've come home. I know everything will turn out okay, no matter how messed up things feel." I force myself to take a deep breath. "More importantly, you make me want to be a better man . . . and when I'm with you, I feel like I'm already on my way."

Jane's eyes finally spill over. At the sight of tears running down her flushed cheeks, I almost choke up too. I swallow the knot of hope and anxiety and desperate need in my throat. The risk that most terrifies me still lies ahead.

"I know I've made more than my fair share of mistakes. But if you'll let me, I'm willing to work hard to fix them, because . . ."

One final click. Exhibit F is a photo of an elderly couple sitting side by side on a porch swing, her gnarled hand resting atop his, their smiles content.

"I want you to be the *last* girl I ever love too."

I turn off the projector and set the remote on the table. The ball is in her court now. Whatever happens, at least I can tell myself I tried.

Her eyes lock with mine, and the room stays completely silent. Then she stands up.

Jane steps forward, slowly at first, then with more purpose as she heads straight for where I'm standing at the front of the room. At first, I can't tell if she's pissed at my very public apology, but then I meet her eyes, and everyone around us fades away. She stops right in front of me.

"What the hell was that?" she asks, her voice soft and without any hint of anger.

"That was me winning you back." My voice has more confidence than I feel.

She shakes her head, a smirk shaping her lips. "Everything's about winning with you, isn't it?"

I wrap my hands around her upper arms, carefully at first, to be sure she doesn't pull away. But when her mouth lifts in a smile, I tug her close.

"Damn straight it is, baby."

Jane only rolls her eyes. "You're an idiot. You know that, right?"

"I'm an idiot who loves the shit out of you. And I won't lose you again."

The time for exchanging words is done, because I pull her to my chest and our lips meet with a trembling sigh. And then I'm kissing Jane, kissing her like my life depends on it, and her father's not standing ten feet away. Her lips part, and I greedily devour her, sucking on her tongue when it reaches out to taste mine.

The rest of the team erupts in cheers, clapping and whistling and hooting like we just won the Super Bowl. But I barely hear the ruckus. I'm holding my dear Jane tight, and this time, I won't let go.

• • •

"You're crazy, you know that? That presentation back there . . ." Jane's tone is stern, but her mouth draws up in a hope-filled smile.

I shrug and take a step closer. "I want you back, Jane. Simple as that."

We're in her apartment—her place is closer to the training facility, and the desire to be someplace quiet as soon as we left the meeting were the main driving factors.

"Before this happens . . . can we talk?"

"Of course we can. Whatever you want."

She takes a deep breath, steadying herself.

"Twice now I've given you my heart, and twice you've tossed it aside."

I swallow, the lump in my throat the size of a damn football. "I know. And we can both agree that it was completely my fault and I was wrong. I'm sorry. I promise I won't fuck this up. Trust me one more time?"

She doesn't answer right away. But something in me knows she won't deny this. This connection we have. But there's one thing I'm not sure of—will she agree to trust me one more time?

My grand public display in front of the entire team was . . . sweet, I hope, if not a little awkward. But it was sincere, and I could see the emotion in her gaze as she watched me in that conference room, working out in her head if she was going to crush my heart, or love me forever. I hoped like fuck it was the latter.

For me, it wasn't even a choice. She's mine, like it or not. No woman has even come close to measuring up in the last ten years. I tried to move on, tried to get over the crushing blow of our break-up, but she's always held a piece of my heart. My feelings for her have never faded.

And I know with certainty that no one has

made her feel so deeply, even if the emotions were as wide-ranging as love to hate. But I once heard that the opposite of love isn't hate. It's indifference. And if there's one thing she's never felt for me—it's indifference.

She places her soft palm against my cheek and nods. "You've got one more shot, big boy. Don't blow it."

My lips meet hers. I intend for the kiss to be slow, sweet, exploratory, but the moment she kisses me back, it's like throwing a lit match into a can of gasoline. We combust. I groan and bring my hands to her jaw, deepening the kiss when she opens for me. And then I walk us backward toward her bedroom, because the need to show her how much I love her is a physical ache.

I don't stop until we've bumped into the edge of her bed, and then I break from her sweet mouth only long enough to peel her shirt off over her head and tug down her skirt. Jane's fingers fumble with the opening to my pants, and *fuck*, I've never wanted her more than in this moment. But I need to slow the hell down or this will be over before it's even started.

"So, tell me about this date you went on."

Jane chuckles and rolls her eyes. "While we're naked? Really, Wes?"

Part of me knows that we should be talking, taking things slow, that we should be making peace and figuring out where we stand. But the other part of me—namely the raging erection between my legs—knows there will be time for that later. The fact that my little impromptu presentation won her over is a fucking miracle.

"Did you kiss him?"

She blinks up at me, stroking my chest. "Would it matter?"

I clench my teeth. "Guess not. As long as you know one thing."

She tilts her chin up toward me. "What's that?"

"That I'll be the last man you ever kiss."

Yeah, I'm cocky, but fuck it, it's the truth. I want to be the last man who ever has the pleasure of feeling her lips.

Her eyes widen slightly at my serious tone. "Are you . . . proposing?"

I touch her bare arms, trailing my fingertips from her shoulders to her wrists. "Not yet. I'm missing a certain piece of hardware, but you should know my intentions, baby."

"Which are?" She's fighting off a smile.

"To marry the shit out of you. Build a home with you, to make babies. Worship you like the goddess you are for all the days of my life."

I swear I see the hint of tears in her eyes before she blinks. "I love you, Wes."

I lean down and press my lips softly to hers. "I love you too. Always have. Sorry I was such a jackass."

"Well, you have been hit in the head a lot," she whispers, her lips nearly touching mine. "And for the record, no, I didn't kiss him. He didn't even like football."

I chuckle, but once our lips meet, it's like all the electricity in the room zaps to life at once. The time for talking is done. She makes a needy noise in her throat when my tongue reaches out to meet hers.

Then she's reaching down, taking my cock in her soft hand, stroking me in long pulls . . .

And that's the game, folks.

The muscles in my thighs tremble as I guide her onto the bed. Once her head is on the pillow, I waste no time, kissing a path down her body until I reach my new favorite place, the spot between her thighs. It means she can't reach my cock anymore, but that's fine, because I intend to make this all about her. As I plant wet kisses all over her tender flesh, Jane whimpers and squirms beneath me.

"Need a taste of this, baby," I murmur before lowering my mouth to her in earnest, sucking and nibbling and kissing my way along all the spots that make her moan.

It takes only minutes before she's moaning my name and coming apart under my tongue. I have to reach down and wrap a strong fist around the base of my cock to keep from going off like a rocket on the Fourth of July.

God, this woman. She gets me more worked up than anyone. Ever.

I reach for my wallet on the floor and extract a condom, but Jane shakes her head.

"No condom."

I meet her eyes, and the emotion I see reflected back at me makes my insides twist.

This moment is huge. Monumental.

I've come inside her before, back when we were stupid fucking teenagers. And I got her pregnant. It ruined everything between us, unbeknownst to me. And yet Jane, with her huge heart and forgiving nature, is telling me that she forgives me. That she really does love me.

My chest feels like it's been split wide open as I align myself with her damp center and begin to push forward.

Heaven. The only way to describe this is *heaven.* My own personal slice of heaven on earth.

"You feel so good," I murmur incoherently as I bury myself balls deep inside her.

Jane makes a noise of pleasure, and I'm lost.

Kissing her neck, I begin moving my cock in shallow thrusts, afraid that if I fuck her like my body craves, I'll come way too soon and embarrass myself. And I want to make this good for her. I have to. She's given me everything.

"More," she says on a groan. "Please."

I can't deny her, and soon I'm racing toward orgasm, but won't let myself go before she comes again.

And holy fucking shit. Fucking her bare? It's the best thing I've ever felt. She's so hot and tight, I have to clench my teeth and focus on the wall above her head in an effort not to come too soon.

Then Jane takes my jaw in her hands and guides my mouth to hers. She tilts her pelvis, meeting me thrust for thrust, and then she shudders, milking me as she climaxes.

I follow her over the edge moments later, my entire body trembling with the powerful release before I collapse onto the bed beside her, breathless.

Damn. I never knew sex could be so good.

"Does this mean we're back together?" I ask, my voice shaking from the intense pleasure still zipping through my veins.

Jane only chuckles. "Shut up and kiss me, you big idiot."

And I do. A lot.

CHAPTER Twenty-one

Jane

There's something about Wes's new place that just feels like home to me. Maybe it's because his building is so close to my apartment, only a few blocks down the street. Or maybe it's the framed picture of us hanging on the wall of the living room, a shot of us kissing on the field at the end of the last practice of the season.

Or maybe, and most likely, it's the smell of chicken parmesan wafting out of the kitchen as the Hawks' MVP, Weston Chase, who is now officially my boyfriend, is hard at work making me dinner.

Yup. That has to be it.

"I can't believe you've never cooked your favorite food before," I tease, taking a good long sip of my gin and tonic. I lean against the kitchen counter, watching the show from a comfortable distance as Wes concentrates on creating the perfect homemade bread crumbs.

He shrugs. "I always get takeout. That, or go home and see my mom."

It seemed only right to let Wes take the reins on cooking the chicken parmesan this time around. Admittedly, it's more than a little gratifying to watch him bring his usual laser focus to the task of breading chicken.

It's his first time cooking in the new apartment, and it's fun to watch him try to remember where he put everything when he unpacked. The entertainment value is increased by the fact that he's wearing the apron I bought him.

I picked it out as a housewarming present when he signed the lease on this place. It was the biggest apron I could find anywhere, but it still looks miniature on his bulky frame, the words DON'T HATE, TAILGATE printed in Hawks red across his broad chest. A corny present, I know, but when he opened it, he smiled like he'd just unwrapped a Rolex, kissing me and promising he'd wear it when he cooked for me in his new place. That was an offer I couldn't turn down, and luckily, I knew just the recipe.

I grin as my gaze drifts down to his tight butt.

"I thought Mom said this was easy." Wes plops the last piece of chicken into the bowl of bread crumbs, flips it over a few times, and sets it gingerly on the baking sheet. He's been at this for almost an hour now, which makes me feel a bit better about how long this recipe took me to complete.

"I bet it is easy." I shrug. "For a couple that doesn't have every takeout place in town on speed dial."

He smirks, wiping his hands on the apron before bringing the baking sheet over to me for final approval.

"*Magnifico*," I say in my best Italian accent. "I'm excited to actually get to taste it this time."

"Yeah, yeah." He rolls his eyes and heads for the oven.

Just because we're officially a couple doesn't mean I've stopped giving him shit about the night he stood me up. But now that we're together, it's something we can joke about, just another bump in our past. If there's one thing being with him has taught me, it's that the past can't always predict the future.

And I can really see a future with him. I can picture us settling down with babies of our own someday, and game days as a family.

While Wes is busy figuring out how to operate his new oven, I get to work fixing him a gin and tonic. I like that they've become our *thing*. I like having a *thing* with him. I measure out the gin to the soundtrack of Wes pushing button after button on his oven, producing a symphony of beeps until he finally manages to set the timer.

"We've got forty-five minutes," he says matter-of-factly, untying his apron and hanging it over the back of a kitchen chair.

As I'm slicing the lime to garnish his glass, I feel his hands cup my hips from behind as he presses a slow, sultry kiss onto my cheek.

"What are we going to do with forty-five minutes?" His lips against my ear send a pleasant shudder through me.

Ten years, and this man still knows exactly how to make me weak.

I giggle as I try to keep my focus on preparing this drink, but Wes's lips are a welcome distraction from my bartending. He trails kisses down my neck to the dip of my collarbone, sliding the strap of my tank top off my shoulder.

"It seems like you might have a few ideas on how to kill time." I pivot to face him, handing him his gin and tonic, which I've somehow made beautifully despite his best efforts to keep me from doing so.

As he takes a long sip, I tuck my thumbs into his belt loops and tug playfully to show that I'm game. He squints at me from behind his drink, silently assessing my intentions, as if they weren't obvious.

I'll make it easy on him. With one thumb, I swiftly pop open the button of his jeans.

"Oops," I whisper, and Wes's smirk matches mine as he sets his glass on the counter.

"Oops?" He challenges me, wrapping a strand of my hair around his finger.

"Yeah, oops."

Wes puts a hand on the small of my back and pulls me flush against him, tilting my chin up with one index finger so that my gaze meets his. "Am I really supposed to believe that was an accident,

Jane?”

“Wasn’t this all an accident?” I ask coyly, gesturing between the two of us. “I never meant to fall back in love with you.”

Wes chuckles, tucking my hair behind my ear. “Me neither, baby. But it’s too late now.”

He presses a tender kiss against my mouth, which turns into a more passionate one, and suddenly we’re a blur of tongues and skin as he carries me to his new bedroom. Soon, we’re tangled together on the bed, and I’m groaning beneath him.

Good God. If this is an accident, it’s by far my favorite one.

Epilogue

Weston

Eight years later

I blow my whistle and form a *T* with my hands. "Halftime! Great work, kids, you're all really improving. Let's take a break and have a snack."

Most of the six-year-olds scurry to the bleachers, eager for treats and attention from their parents. A few get distracted on their way and have to be called over again.

But our little Madison, the only girl on the local pee-wee flag football team, is still doggedly practicing her throw as if she didn't hear a thing. Even the sudden lack of partners doesn't dissuade her; she just heaves the ball a few feet, trots after it, bends to pick it up, and repeats.

God, it's adorable.

I walk across the field to that lone blue-clad figure and squat next to her. My knees twinge in protest.

Now that I'm well into my mid-thirties, all those old football injuries have started coming back to haunt me. Of course, that isn't the only reason—or even the biggest reason—why retiring last year was the right decision. I glance at Jane sitting in the bleachers, her folded hands resting on her swollen belly.

"Hey there, sweet pea. You wanna go see your mom? Get a drink of water?" I ask Maddie.

"No!" Her brow furrowed in concentration, she scoops up the ball and clutches it to her chest, ready to throw it again.

"You're not tired?"

She shakes her head emphatically, the tail of her brown braid flopping around under her helmet's rim. "I wanna play."

"You're not hungry for string cheese and grapes?"

That gives her pause. She frowns down at the football in her hands as if it can answer me for her.

Out of the corner of my eye, I can see Jane with one hand pressed to her mouth, trying not to laugh out loud.

Finally, Maddie starts walking to the bleachers. She's still cradling the football, but I'd rather clean smeared food off it than face the tantrum that happened last time I tried to take it away from her.

I follow her and sit next to Jane. Maddie drops her helmet with a clatter, perches on the ball between Jane's feet, and digs into her snack with gusto.

While Maddie is absorbed, I ask Jane, "You doing okay? Want me to get you anything?"

"Quit fussing," she replies with fond exasperation.

"I'm the husband. It's my job." I brush my lips over her cheek. She's due to pop any day now, and the suspense has been killing me.

She pats her stomach. "You have nothing to worry about. Maddie's birth was a piece of cake, and I'm sure the twins will be the same, I can feel it."

Damn. I love how confident she is. But she's right. We've got this. "That doesn't mean I don't get to take care of you until then." I shift to a teasing tone. "May I offer you some water, then? The finest blankets from the trunk of our car? A foot massage?"

"I'll take that last one . . . *after* we put Maddie to bed tonight." Jane winks at me, sending a lick of heat through my body. "But, seriously, I promise I'm fine." The corners of her eyes crinkle in a smile. She's collected a few faint crow's-feet in recent years, and they've only matured her beauty. "Better than fine. I feel amazing."

We had a little trouble conceiving at first, as happy as we were to try. But after the first few months, I knew Jane was worried, and probably thinking about the miscarriage she had when she was eighteen. But then things came together, and I know without a doubt how blessed I am.

Sighing, I press a soft, lingering kiss to her mouth. "I love you so much."

"Ew," Maddie whines.

Jane laughs. "You don't like kisses?" She sweeps our daughter up into her lap—what little room she has left on it—and peppers her cheeks with rapid-fire pecks until Maddie is giggling and flailing with delight.

I wrap my arms around them both and drop my own kiss on the crown of Maddie's tousled head. I stay like that, enjoying holding my two favorite girls in the world, until my watch beeps to signal the end of halftime.

Maddie tags close behind me as I walk back out to the "fifty-yard" line—which is really at twenty-five yards on this junior-sized field. I toot my whistle again to get everyone's attention.

"We ready to play?" I shout.

Parents put away the snacks while kids trickle down from the bleachers in ones and twos. It's a few minutes until all fourteen are scattered over the turf. I herd them into position—several of them have forgotten that teams switch at halftime—help them put on their flags and helmets, and retreat to the sidelines.

"Remember, blue team is defense now, and red team is offense. Kickoff in three, two . . ." I hit the START button on the game clock and blow my whistle.

One little boy in blue holds the ball while another kicks, misses, tries again, and successfully punts. Almost before the red team's returner catches it, Maddie has already rocketed off and snatched the flag off their center guard.

“Way to go, Maddie! That’s my girl!” Jane whoops from the bleachers.

Our daughter doesn’t glance at her or even slow down; she’s totally focused on carving a path to the ball carrier. But she grins proud and wide, showing her missing front tooth, and my heart could float away on her smile.

Just as I’ve done every day for the past eight years, I think, *Thank God for second chances.*

Also in this Series

Spotting a hooker on a city street corner isn't an abnormal thing.

Me bringing one home? Well, that's a first.

But this girl . . . she's in trouble. And the guy she's talking to isn't someone she wants to go home with.

So I do the exact thing I shouldn't—I offer to bring her home with me instead.

She says this is the first time she's ever done this, which is adorably ironic. Then she proceeds to tell me a sob story about needing money to care for the baby who was left on her doorstep. That's when my stomach starts to clench. I think she may be telling the truth.

So I do what any respectable man would do. I take her home, stopping to pick up diapers and formula on the way, and discover that she was telling the truth all along.

Christ on a cracker.

I should have just kept walking.

I should have done a thousand other things except for barge into her sad life, offer to fix everything, fall for her . . .

Acknowledgments

A mountain of gratitude to all of the readers out there who have bought my books, who have read them and left reviews, and who have messaged me, telling me you enjoyed my stories. I am so grateful to you! I couldn't live without my rock stars Alyssa Garcia and Danielle Sanchez. Thank you both so much. I would be lost without my miracle-working editor, Pam Berehulke. I would seriously be rocking in a corner somewhere. Thank you for being so easy to work with, and for helping make my stories shine.

Last, thank you to my football-playing husband, John, for all the inspiration.

Get a Free Book

Sign up for my newsletter and I'll automatically send you a free book.

www.kendallryanbooks.com/newsletter

Follow Kendall

BookBub has a feature where you can follow me and get an alert when I release a book or put a title on sale. Sign up here to stay in the loop:

www.bookbub.com/authors/kendall-ryan

Website

www.kendallryanbooks.com

Facebook

www.facebook.com/kendallryanbooks

Twitter

www.twitter.com/kendallryan1

Instagram

www.instagram.com/kendallryan1

Newsletter

www.kendallryanbooks.com/newsletter

About the Author

A *New York Times*, *Wall Street Journal*, and *USA TODAY* bestselling author of more than two dozen titles, Kendall Ryan has sold over two million books, and her books have been translated into several languages in countries around the world. Her books have also appeared on the *New York Times* and *USA TODAY* bestseller list more than three dozen times. Kendall has been featured in publications such as *USA TODAY*, *Newsweek*, and *In Touch Magazine*. She lives in Texas with her husband and two sons.

To be notified of new releases or sales, join Kendall's private Mailing List:

www.kendallryanbooks.com/newsletter

Get even more of the inside scoop when you join Kendall's private Facebook group, Kendall's Kinky Cuties:

www.facebook.com/groups/kendallskinkycuties

Other Books by Kendall Ryan

Unravel Me

Make Me Yours

Working It

Craving Him

All or Nothing

When I Break Series

Filthy Beautiful Lies Series

The Gentleman Mentor

Sinfully Mine

Bait & Switch

Slow & Steady

The Room Mate

The Play Mate

The House Mate

The Bed Mate

The Soul Mate

Hard to Love

Reckless Love

Resisting Her

The Impact of You

Screwed

Monster Prick

The Fix Up

Sexy Stranger

Dirty Little Secret

Dirty Little Promise

Torrid Little Affair

xo, Zach

Baby Daddy

Tempting Little Tease

Bro Code

Love Machine

Flirting with Forever

Dear Jane

For a complete list of Kendall's books, visit:
www.kendallryanbooks.com/all-books/

CPSIA information can be obtained
at www.ICGtesting.com
Printed in the USA
LVHW04s2340191018
594246LV00001B/89/P

9 781732 191143